MOO PAK

MOO PAK

a novel .

Gabriel Josipovici

CARCANET

First published in 1994 by
Carcanet Press Limited
208–212 Corn Exchange Buildings
Manchester M4 3BQ

A CIP catalogue record of this book
is available from the British Library
ISBN 1 85754 090 5

Set in Bembo by Koinonia, Manchester
Printed and bound in England by SRP Ltd, Exeter

For my mother

'Me cry there.' Bertrand

On Tuesday I received a note from Jack Toledano asking me to meet him today at the Star and Garter in Putney at the usual time, wrote Damien Anderson. I am used to these notes. Jack does not need to specify the time. If I cannot make it he goes for a walk himself, but I always try to be there because there is nothing better than going for a walk with Jack Toledano. London is a walker's paradise, he says, but you have to know where to go. Paris is for the flâneur, he says, but London is for the walker. The only way to think, he says, is at a desk, the only way to talk is on a walk. Perhaps think is the wrong word, he says, and what I mean is the only way to make something which will cause others to think is at a desk with a typewriter in front of you. I am quite incapable of thought, he says, but with a type-writer in front of me and a nice thick wad of A4 at my right hand I can, if all goes well, simulate thought and stimulate thought. He abhors word-processors. They are, he says, the comic apotheosis of Villiers de l'Isle Adam's famous remark, which should now read: 'Writing? Our word-processors will do that for us.' People are always trying to persuade me to give up my typewriter and adopt an Apple or a Mackintosh or a Toffee or something like that, he said as we walked over Hampstead Heath last July. They try to persuade me that with one of these things I will never again have to go back to the top of the page if I make a mistake, that I can simply remove the offending word or phrase and substitute a new and better one. They do not realise, he said, that there is nothing I like better than to put a new page in the typewriter and start again from the beginning. In fact, he said, that is the only thing I like about writing, the rest is drudgery and anguish. They do not realise, he said, that for me covering the white page for the first time is so frightening and so desperate an act that I can only do it because the alternative is even worse. There must be better ways to go about things, he said on the Heath that day, but unfortunately I have never found them. That is why, he said, it is such a pleasure to put a clean sheet into the typewriter and then simply copy out what I have already written except for the offending word, the offending sentence. The way I work, he said, and if you say it's crazy I have to agree with you, believe me I've tried other ways but this is what's natural to me and this seems to be the way I have to do it, the way I work the only time work is at all bearable is when I have to start again at the top of the page and simply copy what I have already written except for the offending word, the offending phrase. It is strange how authoritative what you have just written in doubt and despair can seem to be when it is there typed out on the page at your side, he said. But when I try to explain this to people who are trying to persuade me to change to an Apple or a Mackintosh, he said, they look at me as though I were mad. They are clearly much more self-confident than I am, he said, they clearly know much better than I ever will what it is they want to say, and they can tap it into their Toffees or their Apples or whatever they are and watch it all come out on the screen. You can play around with the sentences, they say, you can sit there and play with the words and the sentences. But I don't want to play with the words and the sentences, he said, once I start playing with the words and the sentences I will never be able to move forward at all and I will grow less and less sure which of the many possibilities is the one that will suit me best and then I will grow more and more unsure of what best means and of what I was trying to do in the first place and I will probably end up kicking the screen in out of frustration and despair. That is why I gave up writing by hand, he said that day on Hampstead Heath, that is why I turned to the typewriter. In the days when I wrote by hand, he said, I would spend a day playing with one sentence or perhaps one paragraph, turning it this way and that and when I had finally got it to sound as I wanted it to it would be late in the day and I would be worn out and I would leave it with at least the pleasurable sense that something small but significant had been achieved. But when I looked at it the next day, he said, I saw that it was all wrong and clumsy and incoherent and that it was only exhaustion that had made me imagine the previous day that I had achieved something. So I would start again from the beginning and by the end of the day I would feel that I hadn't got very far but that at least I had got somewhere, only to find the next day, and so it went on. That is why I gave up writing by hand and learned how to type, he said. With a typewriter you have to go forward, you have to keep typing, and that was the saving of me. If I switched now to a word-processor, he said, I would be back where I started. I would spend the day moving words and sentences about and never advance beyond the first paragraph. What I realised early on, he said, was that it was only by going forward that I could discover what it was I was trying to say, trying to make. If I stayed with the first paragraph, he said, it wouldn't get better and I would never discover how it could get better. Only the last paragraph can tell you whether you've got the first paragraph right, he said, only the last word can make sense of the first. There is no *mot juste*. he said, at least not till the whole book is more or less *juste*. The search for the *mot juste*, he said, leads to overwriting and dullness and the dreadful proliferation of adjectives. The adjective, he said, is the writer's greatest enemy. People who cannot write and cannot think and yet believe that they adore literature are in love with adjectives, he said, for them literature is synonymous with adjectives, they pass their lives in a bubble bath of adjectives. I, on the other hand, he said, cannot read a book when it is stuffed with adjectives. They make me literally sick, he said. The adjectives and all those other *mots justes*, they stick in my throat and make me want to throw up. It has nothing to do with taste, he said, it has to do with metabolism and physiology. At least, he said, I am not alone in this. The best writers know that adjectives are the death of narrative. That is why Raymond Chandler does not write: 'I entered the room. On the floor there was an enormously thick carpet made of etcetera which etcetera.' What he writes is: 'I entered the room. The carpet tickled my ankles.' His old Olympia semi-portable, which he bought second-hand nearly thirty years ago, and on which he has written ever since, seemed to have reached the end of the road some years ago, Jack said, and he decided that the time had come to switch to an electronic typewriter. The man in the shop showed me all these models, he said, and I only asked him one question: Is it silent? I told him that when I worked I needed absolute quiet and that the humming of an electric machine would drive me mad, he said. He assured me that the model he was proposing was the most silent they had ever produced, and he switched it on to make me hear for myself. And it was true, he said, in the shop it seemed to emit no noise at all. But as soon as I brought it home, Jack said, and installed it in my study and sat down to work, presumably because my study is much more silent than the typewriter shop, I was aware of a low hum, which began as soon as I switched on the machine and stopped as soon as I switched it off. For several weeks I tried to ignore this hum, he said that day on Hampstead Heath, but in the end I had to admit to myself that I would always be aware of it and that I could do absolutely no work so long as it persisted. Not only did the machine hum, he said, but a red light came on when I switched it on and whenever I paused and tried to think about how I should proceed I was aware of that red light shining at me accusingly, reminding me of the fact that I had come to a stop. I grew to hate that red light, he said, I grew to dread it. At first I tried to press on and ignore it because I knew that once I stopped I would be conscious of it and be quite unable to go on, but of course I was aware of it sub-liminally even when I was pressing on, so that my days were spent fighting my own awareness of that red light and my work, not surprisingly, suffered. It was always with something more than relief, he said, that I would switch off the machine and know that the red light was no longer shining. Then, he said, I tried to cover the light with masking tape, and I tried to shut out the hum by filling my ears with cotton wool, but I was always aware of the fact that behind that masking tape the light was shining and I found that it was quite impossible to put two decent sentences together with my ears stuffed full of cotton wool. In the end, he said, I brought the machine back to the shop and got out my old Olympia semi-portable again, and have made do with that, lame and bronchial as it is, ever since. He has often tried, he says, to write with a pen or pencil since he began to work regularly on the typewriter, believing that one should after all be able to write in whatever circumstances one finds oneself, but it has never been any good. Holding a pen in your hand, he says, and forming the letters, you are too close to your own body, and the letters soon turn to doodles, the words refuse to come, the rhythm so necessary to your writing goes. Only an old-fashioned manual typewriter will suit my specific needs, he says, only such an instrument will provide me with the necessary distance and the necessary rhythm for what I want to do. The word-processor and the pencil, he says, are at once too distant and too close, and you never get the feeling that you are advancing, as you do when you take a page out of the typewriter and lay it down on all the other pages you have written and insert a new one and start to cover that as well. Writing, he says, is a means of escape from the self as well as a means of discovery. You cannot discover if you do not let go, he says, and neither the word-processor nor the pen allows you to let go. When Borges was very old he came to London, he said as we strolled through Kew Gardens one day last Spring, and answered questions in public at the ICA. The questions had to be written out and submitted beforehand, so that they could be read out to Borges and he could decide which ones he wanted to answer. One of the questions was why he never wrote about women and if this was because he never thought about them. On the contrary, answered Borges, he thought about women all the time, indeed he wrote, he said, in order to stop himself thinking about them. That is why a pen or a word-processor is no use, Jack Toledano said that day on Hampstead Heath, with a pen or a pencil you cannot escape yourself and your fantasies and why else does one write if it is not to escape from the prison-house of the self and its banalities? Pens are for Victorian novelists, he said, and word-processors are for playful post-modernists. But if I am anything, he said, it is a modernist, neither a sentimental Victorian who pours out his fantasies wrapped up in absurd and melodramatic plots nor a sentimental and cynical post-modernist who tries to give the impression that he has no feelings but wishes only to toy with all traditions and impress his peers and satisfy the fat cat of a publisher who has given him a ridiculous advance, and who very much wants to do all these things but also of course wants to write a book that will make the world love him and crown him with laurels. But for my purposes, he said, the typewriter, the old-fashioned manual typewriter, is the only tool. The manual typewriter, he said that day on Hampstead Heath, is one of the great inventions of the human spirit, like the bicycle, invented at about the same time. He used to cycle a great deal as a boy, he said, and as a young man. But cycling is for students and lovers, he said, it is for those who have said all they want to say to each other in the night and only want to visit churches together and get tired together and end up in unknown inns together. Walking, on the other hand, he said, is for friends. We have walked together over Hampstead Heath and Wimbledon Common, through Hyde Park and Kensington Gardens, Holland Park and Battersea Park, along the river from Putney to Kew and along the river from the Festival Hall to Tower Bridge, along the canal from Limehouse to Regent's Park (surfacing briefly at Islington), in Greenwich and Richmond Parks, and in Epping Forest. There is no better way to talk, he says, than walking through a London Park or across a London Heath, for there is no need to be looking perpetually at maps, as you have to do if you are walking in Scotland or along Offa's Dyke, and there is no need to burden yourself with food and water, you can go as you are and if a rest seems called for there are always benches at hand so that there is no need to sit on the grass and get your trousers wet or end up with ants crawling up your legs and biting you in spots you can't easily get at. At the same time, he says, unlike the strolls you are reduced to taking in a city like Paris or New York, you can walk at a decent pace in the London parks and on the London heaths, at the sort of pace that gets the blood flowing and there is nothing more conducive to good talk than the healthy flowing of the blood in the veins and a decent walking rhythm. Nietzsche perhaps overdid it, he says, as he overdid everything, in his insistence that the only thoughts worth preserving are those that come to one on walks and in his conviction that what was wrong with Descartes and Kant was that they refused ever to get off their backsides. I personally, Jack says, don't know what it means to think, either walking or sitting, but I know that the only way I can make anything that will cause others to think is sitting at my typewriter at my desk and the only way I can talk is walking. A decent conversation, he says, should consist of winged words, words that fly out of the mouth of one speaker and land in the chest of the other, but words that are so light that they soon fly on again and disappear for ever. We don't formulate a thought first and then polish it and finally release it, he said. If we did that we would never get to speak at all. We let it fly, he says, and sometimes it draws something valuable in its wake and sometimes nothing. That is why question time after a lecture is so unspeakably awful, he says, because everyone has been busy formulating their questions long before they have a chance to deliver them, whereas in ordinary life there is no gap between the desire to ask a question and the actual asking. It is better when friends sit across a table talking, he says, or sprawl in armchairs. The familiarity of the room, he says, the fact that they have known each other for a long time, these are the factors that make the conversation flow. They are friends, he says, because they have much in common, unspoken assumptions in common, and because they have much in common theirs can be a genuine argument, whereas the lecturer and his interlocutors share no assumptions, which means that they will always misunderstand each other. But better than sitting at a table, better than sitting in a familiar room, he says, is walking side by side in open spaces which are relatively flat. When two friends are out walking, he says, and one of them says something to which the other does not feel like responding, or asks a question to which the other does not have an answer, then the ensuing silence is not a *heavy* silence, it is not an *aggressive* silence, it is not an *embarrassing* silence, for the rhythm of the walk draws the question up into itself and the silence ceases to be a silence of *emptiness*, it ceases to be a silence of *negation*, and becomes instead an *active* silence, a *living* silence, as the question spreads through the body of the one who has asked as well as the one who has been asked, and is slowly transformed by the rhythm of the walk, until eventually it is answered, perhaps by a further question and perhaps by a story and perhaps by some sort of explanation. Two people cannot walk together and be angry with each other, he says. If they are angry then they are not really walking together, they are each walking alone although they are walking alongside each other. Such solitary couples can often be seen, he says, and they are usually sexual partners, sometimes parents and children, almost never friends. Friendship is the most precious possession, he says, because friendship asks for nothing, makes no claims. Those who are best at friendship, he says, are these whose deepest needs are already satisfied elsewhere, by their sexual partners or their work or their children. On the other hand those who try to satisfy their deepest needs through friendship inevitably end up without any friends at all. That is my one area of disagreement with Proust, he says, that in his anxiety to give due weight to solitude, to sexual desire and to art, he feels compelled to play down completely the importance of friendship and of the conversation of friends. Of course, he says, there are situations in which Proust is right. We have all known instances of would-be writers who spend all their time talking and produce nothing. But I suspect that in those cases solitude would have produced nothing either, and I suspect too that they are not really talking to friends when they engage in the practice of which Proust disapproves so much, they are really talking to themselves with the excuse that someone else is present. I suspect too, he says, that Proust, for all his wonderful descriptions of childhood walks, and such descriptions have never been bettered, never, as an adult, ever went for a walk with a friend. If he had, he says, he would not have said what he did, for there is nothing more exhilarating than a good walk with a good friend, one leaves one's desk at the end of the morning drained and empty and a walk by oneself rarely does more than clear one's head, whereas after a walk with a friend one returns to one's desk with a renewed sense of one's own possibilities and of the possibilities of the material which had earlier brought one to such despair. Of course, he says, when things are going well then there is nothing like a solitary walk to keep it all moving along, but things rarely go well or not for long and then a solitary walk is no help, it often makes things worse and one needs the sensation of someone one can trust, someone who takes one for granted, someone with their own life and views and experiences walking beside one. Pascal was never so wrong, he says, as in his remark that all the misery in the world had been caused by the inability of people to stay quietly in their rooms. I love Pascal, he says, but I love him for his style and his manner and not for his opinions. For there is nothing less conducive to thought and happiness than sitting in a closed room. Whenever we think of thought, he says, we have before our eyes the image of Rodin's Thinker, sitting immense and solitary with his great wise head in his great wise hand and gazing deep into himself. It does not need Gilbert Ryle, he says, to show us that this image is only an image of what those who have never had a thought in their lives imagine the process of thinking to be. It is a great image, he says, precisely because it embodies a myth. But when I put my head on my hand, he says, and look into myself, all that tends to happen is that I fall asleep. There is no such thing as pure thought, he says, there is only a sudden sharp intuition, a stirring of the blood, which you have to coax into shape, into words. Most of the time you do not succeed. Either you cannot find the words or you find words but they are not the right words for the feeling you have had. That does not mean it is purely subjective, he says, you know perfectly well when that stirring of the blood occurs that you have been touched by something quite other than yourself, though that is just about the only thing of which you can be certain. I do not go out walking with you in order to think, he says, I go out walking with you in order to talk. But if our walk has been a good one when I get back home and sit down at my desk what had previously been opaque suddenly becomes clear, what had previously been clumsy suddenly becomes elegant, what had previously been long-winded and heavy-handed suddenly finds concision and clarity. Alone in a room with our head on our hand, he says, we lose any sense of ourselves and of what it is we really want. Only by venturing out, by testing ourselves against the city and its parks and heaths, against our friends with their problems and beliefs, can we find our way back to what it is we want. The trouble with Nietzsche, he says, which is also the trouble with Benjamin, is that deep down they are so very German. I can say that, he says, because my favourite artists are all German, or nearly all. German-speaking it is true, he says, not necessarily German German, but that still means in the ambiance of German culture. Klee was a Swiss, he says, and the Swiss are not notoriously less dull than the Germans, but Klee was Klee, and he had a lightness of touch, a sense of humour, an ability to see his own absurdity, which Nietzsche and Benjamin, not to speak of Goethe and Thomas Mann, signally lacked. Of course, he says, a sense of humour, the ability to see other points of view besides your own, brings its own disadvantage, as we can see with the English, who see so many points of view that the only thing they positively stand for is the fear of solemnity and the dread of being taken in. Yet even the English sense of humour is only limited to a few individuals in every generation and those few seem to be fast disappearing as the English lose their self-confidence and their sense of superiority and become more and more Americanised and brutalised. Today the English still pride themselves on their sense of humour, he says, but in truth there are now few more humourless and sentimental people than the English. Their Puritan legacy weighs heavily upon them, he says, as their Protestant legacy weighs heavily on the Germans and their Catholic legacy weighs heavily on the Austrians and the Spaniards. Beware of a people which prides itself on its sense of humour, he says, there is no-one more pitiful than the bore who tells you in every other sentence that at least he has a sense of humour. And that goes for the Jews as well as the English, he says, and that too I can say, being Jewish myself. Jews, he says, have theories about everything, even humour, and nothing is less funny than a theory about humour unless it is a theory about laughter. By and large, he says, peoples are a disaster and only individuals are worth thinking about. Klee was a Swiss, he says, but that is not what is important about Klee. Kleist was a German and a Prussian to boot, but that is not what is important about Kleist. Rabelais was a Frenchman but that is not what is important about Rabelais. It is only the lowest common denominator of the people we admire which they have in common with their nation and their time, he says. Wordsworth's humourlessness is not what we cherish him for. It is directly attributable to the Protestant culture in which he was nurtured. And the same is true of Goethe and Milton, of Kant and Hegel, of George Eliot and van Gogh. Protestantism, he says, when you come to think about it, has been the blight upon our civilisation. And when it wasn't Protestantism, he says, with its ponderousness, its piousness, its fear of laughter and its smugness, it was Catholicism, with its narrowness, its hypocrisy, its bigotry and its fanaticism. And yet, he says, without Catholicism would we have had Dante and Langland, Evelyn Waugh and Muriel Spark? Without Protestantism would we have had Milton and Wordsworth, Nietzsche and van Gogh? It is the same with the Jews and the Moslems, he says. The worst and the best. But the best is always the triumph of the individual over his age, the triumph of the singular over the mass. Even the Greeks, he says. We are thankfully no longer inclined to bow low before the ancient Greeks, we know too much about the slavery that underpinned the glory of Athens, we know too much about the brutality and the coarseness. But a Sophocles transcended that, an Aristophanes transcended that, a Socrates

Gabriel Josipovici 19

transcended that. I am not talking about genius, he says, you know me better than that. I am talking about the singular transformation of brutality and banality by this individual or that individual. It is they who are our teachers, he says, not ancient Greece or Rome, not the Church or the Synagogue. By a miracle their works have come down to us, he says. We must not forget how great a miracle that is, and how great a miracle is the process which has resulted in our being able to buy the works of Sophocles and Aristophanes and Plato in up-to-date translations and handy editions. The labour of scribes and editors and printers and proof-readers, he says. Because of the work of these dedicated people, he says, we can now pick up the works of singular men and women and read them and listen to them and question them and live with them in greater intimacy than we do even with our own spouses and partners. For a person like myself, he says, with no country and no language to call his own, a life without Sophocles and Dante and Donne and Stevens would be intolerable. They are there to be turned to when one is happy and when one is sad, he says, when one is travelling and when one is sedentary. I agree with Proust in this, he says, that books create their own silences in ways that friends rarely do. And the silence that grows palpable when one has finished a canto of Dante, he says, is quite different from the silence that grows palpable when one has reached the end of *Oedipus at Colonus*. The most terrible thing that has happened to people today, he says, is that they have grown frightened of silence. Instead of seeking it as a friend and as a source of renewal they now try in every way they can to shut it out. Until a few years ago, he says, it was still possible for people to rediscover the value of silence when they left the confines of their homes. Even if their first instinct on coming home was to switch on the radio or the television, when they went out of their front door they had to leave these sounds behind them. But now, he says, they can take their Walkmans along and plug them into their ears and need never be without their dreadful music. It is a drug, he says, and should be treated as a drug. It is more harmful than cannabis and quite as addictive as heroin. At its source, he says, is habit and fear and despair, the fear of silence is the fear of loneliness, he says, and the fear of loneliness is the fear of silence. People fear silence, he says, because they have lost the ability to trust the world to bring about renewal. Silence for them means only the recognition that they have been abandoned. We are truly living in a terminal period, he says, and you only have to look about you to see the Gadarene swine rushing towards the edge of the cliff, their Walkmans fixed to their heads and a dead look in their eyes. And it does not matter if the music they are listening to is Mozart or musak, rock or jazz, since it is all noise for the sake of noise, noise to shut out the silence. How can I love my fellow man, he says, if he is closed to me in this way? How can people find the strength to be happy if they are so terrified of silence? For it requires strength to be happy just as it requires strength to be successful, strength of spirit and strength of will, but despair drains us of our strength. We must think about these things, he says, we must not shy away from them, but at the same time we must ignore them and try to live in the ways that seem best to us, reading our books, taking our walks, talking to our friends. We must not turn our backs upon the world in which we find ourselves living but we must not succumb to the temptation of thinking that it is the only reality or a more real reality. In fact, he says, there is no such thing as reality *tout court*. Wittgenstein was right when he said the world of the happy man is different from the world of the unhappy man. The two may walk side by side down the same street but what they see and hear and what they feel about what they see and hear is totally different. You must know this yourself, he says, how dull and empty the world seems when you are unhappy and how rich and full, how infinitely surprising it seems when you are happy, when you are working well, when you have slept well and taken enough exercise. That is why walking is so important, he says, that is why friends are so important, a walk by yourself can gradually change your mood from one of flatness and depression to one of serenity and even elation, but talking with a friend of long standing, a friend you trust and who trusts you, who has known you in your darkest moments and your blackest moods, in your most triumphant moments and most creative moods, and from whom therefore you need hide nothing, as you expect nothing to be hidden from you, meeting such a friend when you are low, he says, talking with such a friend when you have lost your way, can immediately alter your mood. The combination therefore of a walk and a friend to talk to is not only valuable, for someone like me it is essential, he says, for you it is a pleasant distraction but for me it is essential, different walks with different friends, depending on the season and the day and how my work is going and what mood I am in. He starts off fast, whatever the weather and wherever we are going, so that at first I have to hurry, almost to run, in order to keep up with him, and in the past, when we first started going out for walks together in the parks and on the heaths of London and its environs I felt I would never be able to keep up with him, but either he gradually slows down or I gradually adjust to his pace and quite soon we are walking side by side and I am no longer having to make an effort just to stay within reach of him. Last month we walked in Battersea Park and stopped to look at the poor pathetic animals in what they call their zoo. Jack avoids zoos and will never walk in Regent's Park because of the cries of the caged animals and birds which waft on the breeze from London Zoo, but he makes an exception of Battersea Park. In the past, he says, he made a point of visiting the zoo of every city in which he happened to find himself, his natural curiosity about the variety of animal species and their different grunts and shrieks and howls winning out over his distaste for seeing wild animals in captivity, and so he saw the zoos of Basle and Hamburg and Talin and Odessa and Buenos Aires and Mexico City, but now, he says, the sight of an animal in a cage makes him feel physically sick. He could give money, and does, he says, to save the African elephant and the Indian tiger though he would never give any to save the starving children of Ethiopia or the flood victims of Bangladesh. It's probably quite irrational, he says, but I feel that human beings have brought their woes upon themselves, whereas whole species of animals are dying out because of what we have done to them, and every day countless animals die in atrocious agony inflicted on them by human beings for no other reason than to satisfy their tastes and their greed. In Battersea Park the animals are not in cages but lie about hopelessly on the dried slopes in the heat of our new-style English summers. The urge to anthropomorphise, he said as we left the so-called wild goats and continued on our way, is perfectly natural, and it is only a kind of inverted sentimentality which regards it with suspicion. We are all living creatures, he said, and can learn much about ourselves from looking at a cat, a dog, a rabbit or a giraffe. If you have ever watched a cat stalk a bird, he said, or seen one of those nature films about any of the large cats, a lion, a tiger, a leopard or a cheetah, you will know that the cat is never in a hurry, never does more than it needs to catch its prey, yet when the moment comes to pounce its speed is electric. It moves with such confidence, he said, that the world seems to belong to it. It moves *lazily*, he said as we approached the ponds. It moves quietly. It is as if its whole body was nothing but an eye, an ear. Sometimes, he said, you will see it yawn, perhaps as a sign of nerves, perhaps only out of a massive indifference. And you will know, he said, that it is only very young and inexperienced cats which gnash their teeth in despair if their prey escapes before they have got within range. The mature cat, he said, does not waste any effort on what has not been caught or what, he realises, is not going to be caught. It is as if, the prey gone, even if he has been stalking it for a considerable length of time, he is able instantly to forget about it. He returns to his passivity, his apparent indifference and aimlessness. But when he is once more within range, he said, and motioned me to sit on one of the benches facing the water, the pace quickens imperceptibly and what had hitherto been a kind of passive openness instantly becomes a sharply focussed concentration.

Gabriel Josipovici 23

And when the prey is finally within reach the speed at which the cat launches himself will always take your breath away. But of course it is possible for the cat to switch off at any moment, to return to his previous open passivity. It is as though the energy expended, he said, is never out of control, can always be decreased in a natural and graceful way, so that the whole episode, if he has got within reach of his prey and launched himself and the prey nevertheless escapes, is not so much like a runaway car crashing into a wall and coming to a juddering stop as like a pulse which merely increases rapidly and then decreases just as fast, but always retaining a certain rhythm, and if our attention has been distracted for only a second or two we may have missed the entire cycle and imagine that nothing at all has occurred. The jerk, the spasm, so typical of the human creature, he said, pointing to where two ducks had come flying down through the trees in the direction of the river and were about to land on the stretch of water in front of us, is conspicuously absent from the repertoire of the cat, until the moment of its death. It is as though it moved and had its being in a different air from ours, an air more like water or oil, in which everything was smoothed out, elongated, streamlined. And yet, he said, as we watched the ducks land, letting their legs drop at the last minute and using them as brakes as they skimmed the surface of the water and then, once safely landed, calmly start to paddle as though they had never left the water, the reason why the sight of a cat, and especially one of the large cats, never fails to move us, is because its body is not so totally different from ours and the air through which it moves is in fact the same air as that through which we too move and the ground from which it leaps is the same ground and with the same properties as that on which we walk every day of our lives. That alert passivity, he said, that heart-stopping ability to accelerate and decelerate without any obvious sign of strain, all that is something we feel we know, our bodies feel they know, it is embedded in our dreams and our most secret desires. For most of us it remains and will always remain a dream, but it is given to a few to come close to realising that dream in their actual lives. I remember once, he said, as I was walking on the South Downs near to Brighton, a figure crossed my path about twenty yards ahead of me. It was gone almost before I had had time to take it in but the words that immediately came into my head were: gazelle, runner. I knew it was a man running in white shorts and vest, but somehow I also thought of a gazelle, perhaps because it seemed to be nearly all legs and its movement was so much more graceful and so much faster than anything I had ever seen a man do. What it was I afterwards realised, he said, was Steve Ovett, the Brighton-based runner, in his heyday one of the greatest middle distance athletes the world has ever seen, out for a training run. I realised that, he said, as I walked slowly on and his features, which I thought I had not taken in at all as he flashed past me, came back into my head. I had of course only seen him on television, and television can give you no real sense of the speed and gracefulness of the man and of the almost absurd length of his legs in relation to the rest of his body. Few of us, he said, will ever be Ovetts, but we can all identify with him and with the cheetahs and leopards we have all seen on nature films. The old dream of the body's potential lies very deep inside all of us, he said, yet it also seems to lie very near the surface and is always ready to emerge. So that we have to conclude, he said, and got up and I followed him as he started to walk round the pond and past the beautiful Barbara Hepworth bronze in memory of Dag Hammarskjöld, that all talk of depth and shallowness in relation to feelings and sensations is thoroughly misleading and perhaps we should say that our sense of kinship with the cat lies very far from our minds but very close to the skin that covers our bodies. It was early morning, the park had not been open long, in the smaller parks which are likely to be crowded on a summer's day Jack likes to walk as early as possible so that we can have it more or less to ourselves. On his first visit to Japan, he said as we arrived at the second pond, Stockhausen was struck by how very different the Japanese sense of time is from that of most

Westerners. He noted that people's actions were either much slower or, occasionally, much faster than we are used to in the West, and that it was as though the vast area of intermediate, 'ordinary' time in which we basically live did not exist for the Japanese. Stockhausen recounts, he said, how he watched Sumo wrestlers circling each other for up to five minutes, throwing up bits of earth, hitting their chests with the flat of their hands, going through the innumerable little rituals with which they work themselves up and throw the seeds of doubt in the minds of their opponents, and this went on for so long and so little seemed to be happening that the Western observer might have been forgiven for thinking that nothing ever would happen and letting his mind wander to other things, to his tired legs or to the sight of a beautiful girl, but that would be a terrible mistake, Stockhausen said, Jack said, because quite suddenly the two are locked in combat and one of them has been hurled out of the ring. Once they close, he said, it is all over almost more quickly than the eye can see. One second they are circling each other as they seem to have been doing for an inordinate length of time and the next one of these enormous men is out of the ring and the winner is celebrating. There is clearly a sliding scale, he said, from man to cat, and the Japanese are clearly nearer to the cat than we are. But you must have noticed, he said, how, when you are thinking well you too are closer to the cat than you would normally feel yourself to be. You stalk your prey, he said, you sit there quietly, eyes and ears open yet totally shut off to the sights and sounds around you, and then, when you have the elusive thought in your sights, you fall upon it with the full weight of your concentrated being. Man has spent millions of years moving away from his animal origins, he said, and yet when we are doing what we most want to do we find ourselves closest to the animal in ourselves. The whole story of man's relations to the natural world, of the notion of the animal as Other, he said, as sketched in for the early modern period by Keith Thomas for example in his wonderful book, is part of a larger story, which includes the story of the Jew as

Other, of the native as Other, of the woman as Other, the melancholy demonology of the Christian West and especially of the post-Renaissance Christian West. Fortunately today we are beginning to understand all four, he said, the animal, the Jew, the native and the woman, as essential parts of ourselves which we not only reject at our peril but also positively need to nurture within ourselves. Not out of some abstract ethical imperative, he said and sat down on a bench under a great elm, but because it is closer to the truth about ourselves, our bodies and our desires and the better we understand that truth the better it will be for us. The main strategy of demonisation, he said, is essentialisation – You animal! You Yid! You wog! You bitch! But the fact of the matter is he said, that there are no essences, only diversity and potentiality. For animals, Jews and the rest, he said, are in one sense the reminders of unrealised possibilities in ourselves. Responding to them we discover ourselves. Why, he said, do you think we smile when we see a litter of puppies playing together? Because we can *feel* ourselves at play with them. Why, he said, and leaned forward to look at something in the water, do we crowd round to see a giraffe stretching up to chew a juicy bunch of leaves on the highest branch of a tree? Because we too have necks, he said, which for most of our lives we are not even aware of. The great art historian Meyer Schapiro, he said, once wrote a tiny exquisite article on the grotesque bodies medieval artists were fond of drawing in the margins of their manuscripts. He pointed out how in these drawings tiny human beings play and fight with equally minute creatures whose size they assume without any loss of their essential humanity, and how by reducing man to the scale of these creatures and also by the constant mingling of bodies the artists strip man of his privilege and supremacy and show him as a being among others in nature, sharing in the instinctive mobility of the animal world. It is an art, Schapiro observed, Jack said, leaning back and looking down at his hands, which provides us with a boundless reservoir of humour, play and untamed vitality. No other art in history, Schapiro suggests,

Gabriel Josipovici 27

he said, offers so rich an imagery of the body as a physical engine, as these medieval artists, free from the constraints of classical norms, experiment with the human frame as the most flexible, ductile, protean, self-deforming and self-correcting system in nature. It is no coincidence, Jack said, looking up at me and smiling, that while Swift's first great book was about the absurdity of private languages and yet was itself a veritable encyclopedia of private languages, of grunts and groans and cries and muffled screams, his second great book was explicitly about the human body, about the adult male Western body forced to rethink its possibilities when set beside the very small bodies of one imaginary group of people and the very large bodies of another, and beside the bodies of one of man's closest animal companions, the horse. I sometimes wonder, he said, whether Swift really knew what he was about, what it was he had instinctively cottoned on to, and that is why Swift continues to fascinate me after all these years of work on my book and in spite of the many aspects of his life and personality which put me off and which I find it impossible to relate to. I am still, even now, at this late stage, haunted by Swift, he said, by the young Swift at Moor Park and by the old Swift, a bitter and ironic exile in Ireland tending his trees at Laracor and his garden in Dublin which he called Naboth's Vineyard, though why a Sephardic Jew from Egypt, who has almost by accident ended up living and working in England, should be haunted by an eighteenth-century cleric of the Church of Ireland is beyond my understanding. But perhaps it is just because it is beyond my understanding, he said, that it has provided the necessary stimulus for my work. We are not really interested in what we already know, he said as we sat on that bench by one of the ponds in Battersea Park last month, and we are not interested by definition in what we do not know. Only that which is inaccessible to us and yet continues to haunt us is truly stimulating, he said. The greatness of Meyer Schapiro as an art historian, he said, lies in his remarkable combination of exactitude and generosity, extensive scholarship lightly worn and an almost childish sense of wonder. Elsewhere, he said, one perhaps finds intelligence and scholarship on a par with his, in the work of Panofsky and Gombrich for example, but it is a muffled, self-satisfied, closed kind of scholarship, wholly lacking in real curiosity, let alone wonder, and sadly limited by a late nineteenth-century Viennese aesthetic, humourless, ponderous and, in the last analysis, probably oblivious to the wellsprings of art. The taste of a Gombrich or a Panofsky, he said, is the taste of a good German or Austrian bourgeois of the nineteenth century, and the same is true of Thomas Mann, one of the best and one of the worst writers of the twentieth century, and of Adorno, one of the profoundest as well as one of the silliest critics of our time. I cherish two images of Adorno, he said. First, in the twenties, as a young man, Theodor Wiesengrund Adorno, putting on an imitation of Marlene Dietrich at a party to cries of 'Well done Teddy!', and second, in 1950, turning up at Darmstadt as the spokesman of the Schoenbergian avant-garde only to find that the young Turks of the post-War era considered him and his master old hat and were totally uninterested in anything he had to say. For that summer school, he said, Adorno, so admirable in so many ways, so subtle, so learned, so full of his mission and so humourless, turned up in shorts. There is a photo of him taken at the summer school, standing in his shorts flanked by Stockhausen and Boulez, Pousseur and Nono. He had come to tell the young what direction their music should take, but, as is often the case with the young, they already knew what direction they wished to take and had no use for this intelligent and learned man who unfortunately had absolutely no feel for any music and art that he had not grown up with, only a great many theories about the future direction which music and art should take. In this he was not unlike Thomas Mann, he said, whom he had of course helped with the musical side of *Dr Faustus* when both men were exiled in America during the war. Dinner with Thomas Mann last night, Stravinsky noted in his diary, the poor man would insist on talking about music. That just about sums it up, he said, not only as far as

Mann is concerned, but also as far as Panofsky, Gombrich, Wind and the rest are concerned. Not, he said as we sat on the bench overlooking the pond in Battersea Park that day, that the present batch of cultural gurus is much better. On the contrary, he said, they are far worse. At least Mann and Adorno and the rest had a certain culture, limited by the taste of their time, but deep and genuine for all that, and at least they could write, which is more than can be said for Macherey and Lyotard and their American followers Fish, Fleisch and Greenbaum, who have taken it upon themselves to tell us we live in a post-modern world and that all art that is not post-modern and playful is to be consigned to the rubbish-heap. What has happened to cultural life since the war? he asked, and got up, why does unrelieved banality reign everywhere, even or perhaps especially in the cleverest and most learned? The best lack all conviction, he said as we started to walk away from the ponds, but they turn this lack of conviction into a philosophy for our times, telling us who we are and how we should think and why the past no longer has any hold on us. He took his floppy white hat from his shoulder bag, for the sun was now out in its full intensity, and set it on his head. I associate these with the gardeners of my childhood, he said. Only gardeners and prep-school boys in Egypt wore hats like these. Here where everybody is a gardener everybody wears them. You used to see them on cricketers, he said, but now they wear swanky hats like cowboys which fall off every time they have to run for the ball. That is the modern condition, he said, the best lack all conviction and the worst are full of passionate intensity. It has not changed since Yeats wrote those lines and it seems unlikely to change for a long time or perhaps ever again. Though what is new is the intensity with which we are being told that we should lack intensity. Perhaps, he said, it was always like that, but I doubt it. You have only to look at contemporary portraits of Dante, he said, to see that he for one was certainly full of passionate intensity. You have only to read the plays of Shakespeare to see that the lack of conviction had quite a different meaning for him than it does for our present-day self-serving champions of post-modernism. The case of Shakespeare is a singular one indeed, he said as we turned towards the running track. It took me a long time to appreciate Shakespeare, he said, perhaps one can never fully appreciate him. To come to terms with him, he said, one has to rediscover how it is possible to be at once totally committed and yet always able to see the other side of things. It is not by chance, he said, and turned abruptly in the direction of the English Garden, that Shakespeare was a dramatist and not a writer of epic like Spenser and Milton or a writer of novels like Fielding and Richardson. You cannot write an epic unless you have a strong view of the world and you cannot write a novel in the style of Fielding and Richardson unless you have strong moral convictions. Shakespeare, he said, had no strong views and the search for such views in his plays is doomed to fail. He worked in a form which had no place for the first person, he said, and no worries about the sources of inspiration, such as haunted Marlowe or even Jonson. It is hardly possible for a thinker like Wittgenstein to respond to an artist like Shakespeare, he said. Wittgenstein, for all his understanding of the nature of the fragmentary, for all his awareness of the co-existence of an infinite number of different language games and different forms of life in the world, was still too much the product of fin-de-siècle Vienna, with its myth of the solitary genius and its absurd overvaluation of Schumann and Schubert, not to speak of Mendelssohn and Wolf, charming and often moving minor composers though they are. Nevertheless, he said as he led the way into the English Garden and found a bench in an alcove under the wistaria, Wittgenstein was *singular* in a way Panofsky and Gombrich and the rest of them can never be. Everything he wrote breathes forth his singularity, the inscape of the man as Hopkins would have put it, the jagged thing that is him and him alone, and in the end that is the only thing that counts and we would be the poorer had we never encountered him. Not less knowledgeable or less clever or less *au fait* with this and that, but simply poorer in spirit. Everything I tried to do as a teacher came back to that, he said, to make these young people grasp the fact that the only thing worth while is the feel of the unique. What the poetry of Wordsworth has to give you, he said, is not the ideas but the *feel* of Wordsworth – which is not of course to be equated with the man Wordsworth. What the poetry of even a minor writer like Herrick gives you is the *feel* of Herrick. And why is this feel so important? he asked, taking off his floppy white hat and stuffing it into his shoulder bag. Because it is the only way we can be made aware of the fact that there exist a myriad possibilities for the human animal, that what we had previously thought of or rather taken for granted as *limits* are in fact nothing of the sort. I think of the great writers, he said, not as great teachers but rather as humble spades and hoes, which help to break up the solid ground, the apparently arid ground of our imaginations, and prepare it for the planting and subsequent growth of the seeds of our own imaginings. If we are prepared to read properly, he said, which means to read patiently, to allow silence to surround our reading, then we will learn this lesson, not as one learns the seven times table but as one learns to somersault from a standing position. One discovers that there are potentialities there within us of which we had never dreamt, for we had mistaken the arid soil for the way things are. To treat the writers of the past as fuel for political views or aesthetic views or epistemological views, he said, is not only to murder them but to murder ourselves. Literature, he said, does not teach us ethics, it does not teach us politics, it does not teach us linguistics. It teaches us gymnastics. I do not mean that it teaches rhetoric, he said, you know me well enough to know that I do not mean that at all. The gymnastics of the spirit, he said, has little to do with rhetoric, though rhetoric, properly understood, can help train us for such gymnastics. But who nowadays is prepared to read the writers of the past as they should be read? Who is prepared to make a space in which we can properly pause and listen? Our students are bombarded with ideas and information, he said, their natural insecurity is exacerbated by teachers who claim to be giving them the key not just to their own lives but to the meaning of the universe and of history. They are enjoined to be morally and politically correct, which means to stop thinking for themselves, to stop feeling for themselves, to look over their shoulders all the time to make sure they have not stepped out of line, and to become part of the herd, with all the comfort and self-satisfaction such an attitude entails. You have to be a teacher, and especially a teacher of literature today, he said, to grasp the extreme and utterly banal morality of the young, and especially of the English and the American young. They are tediously and humourlessly on the side of all the right causes, he said that day in the English Garden in Battersea Park, they are part of the new Salvation Army which is sweeping through our culture, a bitter and self-satisfied army which has ceased to listen because it is utterly convinced that it is right. When all traditions have broken down, he said, the only thing that can take their place is this shatteringly dull and banal morality, a morality which knows nothing about life because it knows nothing about choice and therefore nothing about cost. For someone like me, he said, coming as I do from quite a different environment and having grown up in quite a different culture, the narrowness and bigotry of the present climate is almost impossible to understand. Of course, he said, I have not lived here for thirty years without developing some theories about why this should be so, but theories are really a way of holding problems at arm's length and every new manifestation of narrowness and bigotry among those who should know better is still difficult to take. No-one is surprised, he said, to find narrowness and bigotry in the downtrodden and the barely literate. Only the most naive, he said, would have been surprised by the success of Hitler with the economically and socially underprivileged in the wake of the trauma of the First World War and in the face of the ineptitude and condescension of well-meaning liberal politicians. What is utterly depressing, he said, is to find it among university students, in a social group that is supposed to be more intelligent and better educated than the average and must know that it is more privileged. The trouble with the English, he said, with the so-called intellectual English, is that they will respond only to what they already know. They seem, he said that day in the English Garden in Battersea Park, to be incapable of relaxing enough to let any new thought or idea disturb their certainties. They are so insecure, he said, that such relaxation is beyond them. It was all foretold, he said, in that masterpiece of prophecy, Milton's *Comus*. Comus, he said, the spirit of the forest, of the forests of Wales over which the English, from their redout in Ludlow Castle, tried to exercise control, Comus is the spirit of Shakespeare, of Chaucer, of *A Midsummer Night's Dream* and *The Canterbury Tales*. He is the spirit of the vernacular, of Shakespeare's fools and their quick repartee, of Skelton and Rabelais, the spirit of the Anglo-Saxon and the Celt. And look at what Milton does to him. He transforms him in his Puritan imagination into an image of evil, the figure of the Tempter, just as, long before, primitive Christianity had transformed the figure of the Jew. By his malign power, he said, Comus, in Milton's poem, turns the virginal lady into stone when she will not submit to him, and it is only by the grace of the spirit of the river, an unconvincing goody-goody type, that she is freed and the tempter defeated. The lady, he said, prefers to be turned to stone than to succumb to the Tempter, just as Milton himself transforms the poetry of Chaucer and Shakespeare into his marble periods. This great poem, he said, is indeed prophetic. And it is often recognised as such by the very people about whom it is talking. But they of course take it as a document about colonialism and repression. Their sympathies are of course all with the repressed, with the spirit of the forest, with the Celt and the living language of the people. But note the irony well, he said. It is those very people, the ones who read the poem in this way, who are compulsively repeating the pattern Milton has put forward. Thinking themselves to be fighting Puritanism and repression in the name of freedom, they demonstrate in the way they do it that they too cannot tolerate what does not fit in with their increasingly rigid systems, they too, turned to stone, try to turn all around them into the same substance. These people are so insecure, he said, that nothing must disturb their certainties. They are so confused, he said, that they cannot bear not to be in total control, dispensing judgements and laying down the law instead of acknowledging mystery and complexity. That is not the way to respond to literature, he said, or to any of the other arts. It is not the way to respond to other people. I do not know why the English are so frightened and insecure, he said. They are terrified of whatever they do not know. If something does not fit in with what they know and believe they at once conclude that it is bad and should be treated with the utmost suspicion. This is just as true of the so-called intelligentsia and of the body of university students who are making a bid to become the intelligentsia of the future as it is of the drunken bands of illiterate youths who roam the streets of our cities, taking comfort in the solidarity of the group and the befuddlement of their minds brought on by drink. Recently, he said, I went to Cardiff to read a story of mine. The story had appeared in an anthology of modern fairy tales and a friend of mine, who had edited the anthology, asked me to come down to Cardiff where the publishers, for some obscure reason of their own, thought they would find a market for their book. When I got to the Arts Centre where the reading was to take place, he said, I found twenty or so young people, mostly girls, and a single older man. When I had finished reading the older man immediately jumped in, for this was clearly why he had come, and said that he himself wrote modern fairy tales but that they were quite different from what I had just read, and he proceeded to tell us the plots of a number of his stories. The chairman interrupted and politely suggested that there were many ways to write and many things to write about. At that point one of the girls blurted out that she too was very dissatisfied with what she had heard. According to how the reading had been billed, she said, she had expected something subversive, not what I had given them. When I asked her what she meant by subversive she said: You know, like so and so and so and so, mentioning two popular female writers. I asked her again to explain to me what she understood by the *word* subversive, and after a lot of humming and hawing she came out with the view that it meant critical of established attitudes. When I pointed out that the two ladies in question seemed themselves to be embodying rather conventional attitudes about the exploitation of women and the beastliness of men and were in my view reinforcing stereotypes rather than subverting anything she got up and walked out. But the ordeal was not yet over, he said. Half a dozen other young women in the audience took up her theme in an even more aggressive and intemperate manner. When I tried to explain to them what the word subversive actually meant one of them said she was not interested in my views. I wondered out loud then why if that was the case they had bothered to come and was met by the response that they had been misled by the title of the anthology and had expected something different. The mind boggles, Jack said as we sat in the English Garden in Battersea Park that morning, the mind boggles at a culture in which to be subversive means to fit in with the latest modish attitudes. On the other hand, he said, the older members of the literary establishment are not much better than those angry and confused girls, though they may at times be a good deal more amusing. When they are faced with something that is difficult or obscure they instantly take refuge in irony and a kind of heavy-handed jokiness. Their patron saint is Dr Johnson, but unfortunately they are a million light years away from the real Dr Johnson, whose common sense and impatience with humbug was so curiously and interestingly bound up with his sense of dread and his tendency to despair. But what his modern so-called descendants fear above all things, he said, is being taken in. That is hardly an attitude that is conducive to good reading or clear thinking. But even that, he said, is not as bad as what we find in America. There it is practically impossible to find someone who does not conform to something or feel the need to be part of some group. In America, he said in the English Garden in Battersea Park as we watched the pigeons washing themselves in the little formal pond, sitting on the edge and dipping their heads quickly in and out of the water, in America we can watch civilisation disintegrating in a morass of good intentions. The conservatives are full of good intentions, he said, and the liberals are full of good intentions. Even the crooks and gangsters are full of good intentions, Jack said, they want to do their best by their families and friends and is that not a noble aim? Nixon was full of good intentions, he said, and so was Oliver North and so was that crazy self-obsessed Kissinger. Graham Greene, he said, a novelist, as you know, about whom I have very mixed feelings, put his finger on it in his best book, *The Quiet American*. The Americans roam the world fucking things up and always from the very best of motives and when they die you can be sure their consciences are as pure as the driven snow, whatever that is. But now, he said, England is rapidly becoming indistinguishable from America and soon Poland and Russia will be indistinguishable from America as well. I came to England, he said, in the last days of its real Englishness, when it was considered indecent to wear tapered trousers because only Teddy Boys wore those, and everyone drank Horlicks, when you could get any book you wanted out of the public libraries and the Third Programme would juxtapose a one-hour reading of the poems of Wallace Stevens with the latest play by Ugo Betti translated by Henry Reed. Since then, he said, the libraries have disintegrated for lack of funds, the Third Programme has given way to what one might call a classical musak channel, and England has become more and more like America and less and less like the birthplace of Langland and Chaucer and Donne and Herbert and Pope and Swift and Wordsworth and Coleridge and Tennyson and Arnold and Auden and Empson. He stood up abruptly and marched out of the arbour where we had been sitting. He stood on the edge of the little formal pond and watched the pigeons flying down and dipping their heads in the water, shaking their wings and then flying off inches from our noses. Then he set off in the direction of the river, pulling his floppy hat out of his shoulder bag and setting it on his head. France is not much better, he said. The bookshops are better, of course, though that is not saying much, even the bookshops of Lisbon are better than those of London, but the current crop of French intellectuals is hardly brighter than their British counterparts and does not even have the leavening of wit and eccentricity which occasionally enlivens the offerings of the British. In Paris, as in Milan and Munich, he said, everything has turned into fashion, there are fashions in books and fashions in food and fashions in plays and fashions in clothes. This year, in Paris and Munich and Milan, he said as we approached the pagoda, the skirt is short and Mao is in. Next year the skirt will cover the ankles and it will be Eastern Europe's turn to be in. All this frightful tide of polluted water, this torrent of cliché and fashionable posturings must be avoided, he said, in England and in France, in Germany and in Italy, if we are to live at all. Otherwise to the dehumanisation of working life by factory repetition and to the dehumanisation of children's lives by video games will be added the dehumanisation of intellectual life. But it is already too late, he said. It has already happened. The horror is already upon us and the only way we can fight it is to retreat into the fortress of ourselves and prepare for a long siege. We climbed the steps of the pagoda and walked round it to look at the river. Despite themselves, he said, cities are remarkable things. Because they are not and never can be totally planned they each have kept a life of their own. We do our best to destroy them, to control them, he said, but we merely transform them. Only writers can do justice to cities, he said, painters and composers are help less before them. Only writers can catch their variety, the multiple layers of time and history that have gone to make up each one. Painters are forced to focus on a particular moment, he said, and some have done it brilliantly, like Dix and Grosz, Hogarth and Richard Hamilton. But writers can give you a

sense of the growth and decay, the variety and unpre-
dictability of cities, can convey the feeling which we always
get in cities that they will escape every attempt to tame them
and to make sense of them. Writers are helpless before the
human figure, he said, but they come into their own in response to cities. They are helpless before the human face.
That is where painters come into their own. A description of
a person in a book, he said, is nothing but an embarrassment,
but it is the very stuff of painting. The painter can convey the
very being of the other, he said as we stood looking at the
river, whether his style is that of Holbein or Auerbach,
Rembrandt or Hockney, but the writer can only do that by
means of his entire narrative, not in a paragraph or two of
description. The more adjectives he uses the less likely we are
to respond to his characters. The tide must have been almost
at the turn for the river seemed a mighty stretch of water and
Cheyne Walk very far away on the other side. But where
cities are concerned, he said, the role of writer and painter is
reversed. Though painters are fascinated by cities and have
been for centuries, even the greatest painters of cities, such as
Ensor, have only ever been able to give us vignettes, or meta-
phors. With writers it is different. Even the oldest literatures,
he said, present us with memorable glimpses of cities, think of
Babylon in the Bible and Troy in the *Iliad*, not to speak of the
Rome of the *Aeneid* and the Pisa, Bologna, Rome and Florence of Dante's *Commedia*. Homer, he said as we went down
the steps of the pagoda and started to walk along the river in
the direction of Chelsea Bridge, Homer was more interested
in cities than the commentaries usually allow. It is true, he
said, that the *Iliad* takes place by the sea and on the plain, but
Hector dies for his city and it is from within the walls that his
wife and mother lament him. The Greeks have come from all
over Hellas, from the mainland and the islands, but the
Trojans are a people with a single city, a people with a centre.
It may be the case, he said, that what lies behind the poem is
a simple raid on a foreign settlement, but the poem as we have
it is much more than that. It is about why those without cities

desire to destroy what they see as an affront to them, high city walls and a settled urban culture. It is about the periphery destroying the centre. It is about the way song always comes after death and destruction in a hopeless and yet triumphant effort to put the pieces together again. Helen, he said, is often said to be an excuse, the excuse the Greeks needed in order to gain wealth by looting the source of wealth. But in the poem as we have it she is an excuse of a different kind. She is the excuse of the nomad for avenging himself on those who are settled. As Attila and his hordes avenged themselves on Rome and the Vikings on Chester and as all the nomads in history, those who followed Tamburlaine and those who followed Gengis Khan, have always taken their revenge on the urban and the settled. In another, lesser poem, it would be Paris, the fop, the womaniser, who would be the representative of the Trojans in a poem of the Greeks. It is a measure of Homer's greatness, he said, that it is Hector, the husband and father and son, who stands for Troy. But it is Rome, he said, which is the first modern city, the first manifestation of the city as the place of the dispossessed and the alienated, of directionless crowds and slums and violence and heat, a place where order and decorum, where tradition and courtesy, no longer have a hold, where old taboos are broken daily and sex haunts the streets, the palaces and the bars. One wonders, he said, given the horror of the modern city, why it should have been such an attraction both to the nomad and to the rural populations. But it was and is. Once the traditions of the countryside start to be questioned, he said, then the timeless patterns of rural existence come quickly to be seen as meaningless repressive rules and only the cities seem to provide the necessary free-dom for self-discovery and self-advancement. The city, he said, is the locus of perversity, not just sexual perversity but what Poe called the Imp of the Perverse, that modern desire for self-immolation as the price of authenticity. Though Rome is the first modern city there are already hints of this in ancient Egypt and Babylon. Thomas Mann, who understood these things, had no difficulty in making Potiphar and his wife the archetypes of modern urban perversity, but it was in Rome that it reached its apotheosis and Vienna, Berlin, London and New York have only been imitations of ancient Rome. Today, he said as we emerged from the park and turned down towards Chelsea Bridge, if we are to retain our humanity we must reinvent ourselves as nomads in the cities of the world, we must be prepared to take what they have to offer and move on. Even the countryside today, he said, is in reality only an extension of the city, not just Weybridge and Basildon but even the villages of Cornwall and Donegal, where radio and television, tourists and hotels, cars and coaches, all make it impossible to live in anything other than a city environment. Even in the Himalayas and the Atlas Mountains, he said, the lonely travellers, the missionaries and anthropologists of the last century have given way to the walking parties and the tourist guides, the package holidays and the souvenirs. No part of the world is free of the city, he said, no part of the World can exist simply in the old ways and according to the old dispensations. I was in Prague last year, he said, and of course the first thing I did was to visit the Alt-Neu Synagogue and the beautiful Jewish cemetery where Kafka is buried. But now he is buried not just beneath the earth of his native city but also beneath busloads of German and Belgian tourists, all with their tour leaders holding up their little flags and all with their cameras pointed at the tombstones and the turf. The day of the solitary visitor is over, he said, we can never find ourselves alone, not even in Tintern Abbey. That is the price we have to pay for the spread of democracy and freedom, for the new freedom to travel where they wish granted to everyone by tourism and the universal use of the motor car. Perhaps, he said as we crossed Chelsea Bridge, that is a small price to pay for these things. Perhaps it is selfish to expect both the advantages of modern travel and the peace and solitude of earlier times. But when you have lived with Kafka all your life and devoured his stories and letters and diaries and poured over books of photographs of Kafka's Prague and meditated endlessly on the singular life of this most reticent of men it is depressing, to say the least, to visit the place at last and find that you have to fight your way through busloads of tourists if you are even to enter the Alt-Neu Synagogue and then to pick your way between them and clamber over them if you are to wander in the cemetery and try to breathe its atmosphere and to think again about what happened to the Jews of Europe in our century. The truth of the matter is, he said, that it can only be by the greatest good fortune that we can nowadays be surprised by the world around us, that we can chance on a part of it that is not already packaged and prepared for our gaze and where we do not come across a mass of our fellow men and women already sampling those packages, photographing them and reading out loud from their guidebooks. The element of surprise has gone, he said, and now we realise that it is the most precious thing in the world. Everywhere today, he said, people travel to have confirmed for them what they already know and take photographs to remind themselves that they have really been there. They travel in groups and with strict timetables to adhere to, for their time is limited and everything has to be taken in. That is why, he said as we waited to cross the road, it is necessary for those of us who are aware of the enormity of the disaster to keep our minds open, to let our legs take us where they will, to leave the premarked routes and expect everything and nothing. For if the unexpected has disappeared from the wild and lonely places of the world it is still everywhere about us, if only we can see it. He does not have a phone and will not divulge his address. But he sends little notes: Friday RFH or Thursday a.m. Legless Ladder. If I cannot make it he no doubt walks by himself. On other days perhaps he walks with other friends, to whom he has sent his little notes, but he does not talk about them to me and I am sure he does not talk about me to them. Those who see eye to eye with us on the really important issues are precious, he says, we must overlook the little things about them we may find distasteful or laughable or even shocking, because there are not many of them in the world. Without them, he says, we would be lost, and when one of them dies or settles abroad or disappears from our life for one reason or another it is as though we had lost the use of one of our limbs. That is why certain authors are so precious to us, he says. Dante. Stevens. Kafka. Proust. I can walk with them whenever I want, he says, they always have the time to accompany me, they will never plead a prior engagement or a piece of work that must be finished and they expect nothing in return. Moreover, he says, they are people with whom I am never ashamed to be seen. They have the dignity and integrity we look for in all whom we meet. They make no concessions to the world and yet they are always the essence of courtesy and politeness. They are content to listen, he says, but when we give them the chance to speak their utterances are clear, precise, witty and profound. We do not sufficiently appreciate the miracle of the book, he says. I can go out for a walk with a volume of Dante or Wallace Stevens in my pocket and I can take it out and read it whenever I want. Is that not a miracle? That he who never knew me can speak to me like this? That I who never had the chance to know him can engage in conversation with him at any time of the day or night without feeling that I am intruding or pestering? Our friends enable us to live, he says, and to fulfil whatever we were set on this earth to fulfil. But by the nature of things, he says, there cannot be many with whom we feel totally at ease and whose ideals and ambitions, whose appearance and manner of speaking we can respect and admire. Most of the time, he says, even those we had thought to respect and admire sooner or later reveal that they are more interested in success than in integrity or else they turn integrity itself into a form of self-advertisement. Look at the difference between someone like Beckett and a wholly alien and repugnant figure like Sartre, he says. When Sartre was offered the Nobel Prize he ostentatiously turned it down, so that he would be seen as The Man Who Turned Down the Nobel Prize. But when Beckett was offered it he accepted it, turned the money over to charitable institutions, and disappeared to Tunisia, refusing to speak to reporters. You can strike a man as you strike a piece of silver, he says, and then listen to hear if he rings true. Sartre never rang true, he says, he did not ring true in the Resistance and he did not ring true over the Nobel Prize, so it is no surprise that his work does not ring true either. But the more one learns about Beckett, he says, the more of a piece one finds him, and the more one strikes him the purer he sounds. How can you trust an artist, he says, how can you accept him in his work as a friend and a companion on life's journey, if you see him posturing before the press and on television, reading out the most private portions of his work and answering the inane questions of presenters and interviewers who have got where they have because of their cynicism and opportunism? I myself, he says, I have to admit, did once agree to answer questions on the radio about a book of mine, and do you know the first question the interviewer asked me? He asked why I wrote such difficult works. The very first question and he asked why I wrote such difficult works. I didn't have the presence of mind to reply as I should have, unfortunately, but only meekly asserted that what I wrote did not seem difficult to me and that anyway a little effort on the part of the reader might make the act of reading more enjoyable. The inanity of his question took me aback, I have to admit, he says, and I still wake up sometimes feeling haunted by the fact that I let him get away with asking me a question like that. Every day we see the spectacle of famous writers who go on television and speak to their appalling interlocutors about the deaths of their spouses and their brothers and sisters and then read from their newly published work about the unspeakable pain of the deaths of their spouses or their brothers and sisters and if one criticises them in any way they put on an injured expression and insist that since they live by their writing they need as much publicity as they can get in order to sell as many copies of their work as possible in order to feed their families. It never strikes them, he says, that they do not need to live by their writing, that there are other ways to make a living, even for writers, and that what they do in public gives the lie to what they say in their books. It never strikes them that in the long run their work will only be read because of the quality of being that emanates from it, he says, and that by their actions in front of television cameras and with their unctuous interviewers they are demeaning themselves and their art as well as the dead about whom they are so ready to speak, though the long run, they probably feel, can take care of itself and what they care about is fame and wealth in the very short term. I am not saying that the best artists are saints, he says. They are no more saintly than butchers and bakers and what we know of the lives of artists suggests that many if not most of them have been bastards. I am merely saying that in our modern publicity-conscious world the temptations are more insidious than perhaps they were in the past, and that what media people want above all is to see artists doing the dirt on art and thus confirming them in their world-weariness and cynicism. These people are themselves so bitter and feel themselves to be such failures, he says, that what they enjoy above all else is the sight of writers denying by their public actions and behaviour what they seem to be asserting in their work. Shakespeare and Milton long ago understood what this is all about, he says. Angelo lusts after Isabella in *Measure for Measure* partly because she is so beautiful and so pure, everything he is not, but partly too because if she accepts his offer her purity will have gone for ever. Iago wants to destroy Othello simply because he cannot bear that such an idealist should succeed in his life's project. Isabella and Othello are, as they stand, he says, living reproaches to their tormentors, just as Eve is to Satan in *Paradise Lost*. The old theme is played out again and again in Dostoevsky's novels too, he says, most starkly perhaps in *Notes from Underground*, where Dostoevsky is able to bring out all the dizzying paradoxes of the situation without any need to worry about plot: the Underground Man desperately wants Lisa the prostitute to redeem him by demonstrating that a beautiful spirit such as hers does have a place in the world, but she can only do this for him if he is able to prove to himself that she is a real person like himself and therefore not a beautiful spirit. I put it like that, he says, to show how close to kitsch the whole theme is; nevertheless in the hands of a Shakespeare, a Milton, a Dostoevsky, it escapes from kitsch because it touches honestly on modern man's impossible and contradictory needs and desires. I am not saying that the television and radio interviewers and anchor men of arts programmes are Iagos and Satans and men from underground, he says. For one thing they lack the self-awareness of these characters. Many of them actually think that they are encouraging the arts, he said, they pat themselves on the back and give themselves full marks for bringing the arts to a wider audience. But in fact they are destroying art because they are insidiously destroying the integrity of artists. But next time you watch or listen to such a programme, he said, bear in mind *Paradise Lost* book nine. Milton, he said, thou shouldst be living at this hour. We were walking along the Embankment from the Festival Hall to Southwark, with the dome of St Paul's clearly visible across the river. Some time ago, he said, I saw V. S. Naipaul on television, talking about a book of his I had particularly admired, *The Enigma of Arrival*. Perhaps you know it. I was drawn to it because its subject was one I myself was familiar with, the arrival and settling into this country of a foreigner. Not only that. Whilst most immigrants settle in cities, Naipaul, like me, chose the countryside, and he conveys with wonderful slowness and precision the new arrival's sense that he has come to a place which has not changed for centuries and in which all the other inhabitants are deeply rooted. Only he himself, he feels, is without roots here, a stranger who has been dropped by the whims of fortune in this spot and no other. But gradually he, the stranger, comes to understand that no-one is rooted, that nothing is unchanging, that everything is in motion and always has been, though for each element in the landscape there is a different clock: the next door neighbours only moved here six months ago; three weeks earlier tragedy struck that family down the road; the path through the woods behind his garden did not exist five years before and will be macadamised the following year. The book ends, he said, with the death of the narrator's sister and then, hot on the heels of that and totally unexpectedly, of his brother, both movingly recounted. Movingly, he said – we had turned away from the river to have a look at the repairs being made to Southwark Cathedral – because told in so restrained and quiet a way, so that the personal grief and admirable human qualities of the mourner emerge with full force. The book, he said, is for some strange reason called a novel, but Naipaul does not hide that it is plain autobiography. And when he was asked to read an extract from that book, in the course of a television interview, he chose precisely this section to read from, thus turning something deeply private into a form of rhetoric and implicitly asking the viewer to witness how moved he was and how terrible was his misfortune. I have no doubt that Naipaul is an admirable man, he said, and I have no doubt that he suffered greatly at his tragic double loss. But his reading out the passages which deal with this on television, as though asking us both to sympathise with his plight and admire his writing, I found deeply distasteful and symptomatic of our modern culture. Perhaps Dante and Swift and Kafka were lucky, he said as we entered the deserted cathedral, they never had to endure the temptation of what is called media attention. Perhaps if they had been subjected to it they too would have succumbed, but somehow I doubt it. After all, Beckett did not succumb, Bernhard did not succumb, Pinget has not succumbed. I can go on reading and rereading their work with the profound sense that they are true friends, he said, and that like St Christopher whose image adorns the outside of so many of the little chapels in the Alto Adige where I used to take my holidays, they will carry me on their shoulders when the waters churn and boil at my feet. It will not do, he said as we examined the roof bosses laid out on the floor against the wall near the entrance to the Cathedral, to insist on a clear separation between the artist and his work. I cannot separate the smugness, the self-congratulatory strain in Thomas Mann from my reading of his novels, nor the cold arrogance of Brecht from his poems and plays. That does not stop me being moved and sometimes overwhelmed by the novels of Thomas Mann and the poems of Brecht, but it means I can never feel that they are true friends. And that has nothing to do, he said kneeling down to take a closer look at the heads, carried down from the roof during the repairs and laid out there for visitors to examine, with the facts of their lives as we may read them in their biographies. It leaps at us from their fiction and their poetry. It is their fiction and their poetry that oozes smugness and cynicism, and the biographies only confirm what the fiction and the poetry have already told us. I am not saying either that Dante and Swift and Kafka were perfect in every respect, he said, standing over me and waiting for me to finish looking at the bosses, I am well aware of their anger, their vanity, their pride and their masochism. But none of this matters, he said as we moved on up the nave, because they knew themselves and they suffered for their weaknesses and they behaved with dignity in public. We have got things upside down, he said, when we castigate a poet like Larkin for what we subsequently learn about his private life while we condone the obscenity of writers appearing on TV to tell us how much they suffered at the deaths of their loved ones. Swift's life was as tormented and romantic as that of Keats or Hopkins, he said, yet you can go through all five huge volumes of his collected letters and you will never find him talking about it except in the most dignified and objective manner. Of course, he said as we peered into the newly-built restaurant, this makes the letters pretty dull compared to those of Keats or van Gogh, but there is a kind of fascination in that very dullness. Pope's letters are more interesting to us today, he said as we emerged once more into the daylight, but then of course Pope was more of a Romantic, was in some ways the very first Romantic. You never find in Swift what you find so often in Pope, he said, and what is perhaps the hallmark of the Romantic sensibility, the assertion that *words fail him*, that *his heart is too heavy* for him to speak. Where Swift is concerned everything can be said and said clearly, if the writer is up to the challenge. That is why it is so heart-rending to read in his last letters how he finds his memory failing, writing that he does not remember what he said at the start of a letter or what he wanted to say before he began, that he has lost the ability to string words together in a simple sentence, he who once wrote the most extraordinary sentences in English literature, that he has lost the ability to find rhymes, he who had once been able to find rhymes for just about everything. But that is his fault, the fault of his body and mind, he insists, it is not the fault of the world or the language. Today every second-rate artist knows how to say that he is so overwhelmed with emotion that he cannot speak, that there are thoughts that lie too deep for words and tears, and then to go on radio and television and repeat all that. Swift is like Mozart, he said, Pope is already like Beethoven. All the great quartets and trios of Beethoven, he said, lament the fact that music cannot penetrate to the heart of sorrow, they reach out towards it and then fall back in despair. That is the Romantic legacy, he said as we crossed Blackfriars Bridge and went down again on the other side, that is the subtext of every piece of sentimental film music and of every second-rate poem and novel of our times. Beethoven carries me into the depths of myself, he said, but Mozart, like Swift, makes me proud and happy to be alive and human. We owe it to ourselves, he said, and stopped to look at the river, not to society or to anyone else, to behave with honour and dignity as far as we possibly can. With dignity, he said, not pompousness or smugness or pride. Above all, he said, not to lecture others on how they should live or tell the world how much we are suffering because our brother or sister or wife or daughter has died or six million Jews have been killed or the poor and helpless have always been treated appallingly by those in power. Is it not striking, he said, and we began to walk again, that it is rarely those who have endured victimisation who are hot for revenge but only those who have escaped unscathed? It seems that their guilt at their good fortune presses them to evince more sorrow and anger than the victims lest they should appear to be uncaring. My mother, he said, who endured the war in France and whose hair turned white at the age of thirty-four as a result, was always of the opinion that we should forget what had happened and get on with building for the future, while those the war did not touch still cry out for the perpetrators of atrocities to be brought to justice, as though imprisoning a few sick old men on evidence that can never be secure would bring back the millions who died. Look at the case of Demianjuck, he said, sentenced to death in Israel for war crimes he swears he did not commit and now evidence seems to suggest that he may have told the truth after all and they may have got hold of the wrong man. But it is not the question of the reliability of witnesses so long after the event that is really at issue, he said, it is the continuing desire for retribution on the part of those who did not themselves suffer, and it is the obvious fact that nothing can make up for what happened then and that even if they got hold of the real culprits there would always be a yawning gap between whatever sentence could be inflicted on them and what it was they did. To turn it all into a question of law and punishment is the best way of ensuring that the whole business is wrapped up and forgotten. Nothing that is done after the event can atone for a single murder, he said, so how could anything atone for these millions of callous and brutal murders? If there is anything I loathe more than calls for the murderers to be brought to book, he said, it is the anguished debates about the theology of Auschwitz that so-called intellectuals go in for these days. That is the real obscenity, he said, theologies of the Holocaust and conferences on the Holocaust and televised debates on the Holocaust. It is obscene, he said, to see our leading so-called intellectuals making themselves feel good by finding words to say that what happened then lies beyond words and can never be spoken. It is obscene, he said, and an insult to those who suffered and died. It had begun to drizzle and we took shelter in one of the smart and yet somehow shoddy cafés that have sprung up all along that stretch of the Embankment. It was empty, as these places always seem to be, and we sat down at a table by a window, though the window only gave on to the gallery, with its empty shops and To Let signs. There is no such thing as collective memory, he said, there are only a multitude of individual memories. When a politician evokes collective memory, he said, then it is time to beware. Nationalism, he said. Patriotism. All those old monsters. You can see today how quick they are to resurface. Collective memory is collective amnesia, he said. Our memories are personal or they are nothing. They are not uniform. They are not consistent. They flicker into life and then subside again into the dark. As Proust understood, and had the patience and clarity of mind and the literary skill to convey. We are like fish, he said. We swim in a sea of memories, but they only extend a few feet all around us. Cross that boundary, he said as a waiter appeared with a menu, and we are in new territory, unknown realms. The problem for each of us and perhaps for whole nations like the Germans today, he said, is how to find the balance between too little and too much. Too little memory and we cannot advance because we have floated free of ourselves and of our past and there is no solid ground on which to set our feet. Too much and we cannot advance either because we are stuck in the mud of the past and unable to raise our feet. We need memory, he said, but we must not make a fetish of memory. We need memorials and days of remembrance but we must not imagine that they will solve our problems for us. Like everything else, he said, there are no universal guidelines here, let alone universal panaceas, everyone must negotiate for himself between the Scylla of forgetfulness and the Charybdis of remembrance. In older cultures, he said, in the Christianity of the Middle Ages and in traditional Judaism and Islam, the liturgy regulated the uses of memory, but with the passing of tradition we are like creatures who have emerged from the water where we were born and had spent all our youth and who do not know how to adapt to land and to the air we now have to breathe. There is a letter of Kafka's, he said, an early letter to Brod, in which this inability to adapt to an environment in which air and not water is the medium, is caught with frightening clarity. Kafka writes that now it is summer and he is on vacation he feels full of energy but does not know what to do with this energy. His arms are too long, his legs too far away from him. In a kind of despair he wanders through the streets and squares of Prague, swinging his arms, twisting his torso, raising his legs too high, trying in effect to find a set of gestures that will correspond to his feelings but no doubt looking like a madman to those who come across him. That letter, he said, sums up not only everything that Kafka's life and writings are about but the situation in which we all find ourselves in the two centuries since the French Revolution, when we feel that everything is possible but that there is no way of knowing what to do or how to do it. The shadow of Napoleon haunts the nineteenth century, he said, because in a secular age, when no citizen is in principle debarred from the highest office, when even a simple Corsican boy can become Emperor of Europe and any peddler a millionaire, there seems to be no reason why we should not all realise our dreams. Since, however, for one reason or another, few of us do so, most people only taste the bitterness of what they see as personal failure caused by bad luck and the machination of others. But before you can realise your dreams you must know what those dreams are. Not all of us, he said, want to become Emperors or millionaires, but all of us want happiness and fulfilment. But from which direction is that happiness and that fulfilment to come? What do I have to do to achieve it? I am ready and willing to do anything, and I have the energy and the determination to carry through whatever I set my mind to – but how to start? What direction to take? Where to plant my feet for the first big shove? Because these questions go unanswered, he said, we feel we are flailing the air, we feel, when we are young and strong, an excess of energy which cannot be channelled because we do not know where to find the channels, a need to speak which is constantly frustrated because no language seems adequate to our needs and desires. The pathos of our relations to animals in the modern world, he said lies in this, that animals seem not to experience this sense of frustration and that animal languages always seem adequate to the animal's requirement. On the other hand, he said, we see in the eyes of some pet dogs and in the eyes of all caged beasts a melancholy, a resignation, which suggests to us that they too would like to be elsewhere and would like to speak so that we could understand them. It is a long story he said, this story of the relations between man and beast. The oldest tales speak of talking birds and fish, of magic rings and the like which allow us to understand the language of the animals. In Homer himself we have the first and perhaps most moving account of the relations between man and dog. When Odysseus comes back home in disguise the only one to recognise him is the dog Argos, who lies in the dung outside his house, covered in vermin because no-one looks after him now that his master is gone, and who, when Odysseus appears, immediately starts to wag his tail and drop his ears, even though, says Homer, he no longer has the strength to get up and approach him. But Odysseus, disguised as a beggar, notices him and sheds a secret tear, before asking the shepherd Eumaeus why he lies there in the dung, so uncared for. When the master of a slave goes away, Eumaeus replies, the slave loses his worth. The two men enter the house and Homer quietly adds, in that remarkable even tone of his in which the most devastating things are said: But as for Argos, the fate of black death seized him straightaway, when he had seen Odysseus in the twentieth year. And we never hear of him again. The café, the whole gallery, remained empty, not even the sound of a footstep echoing across it. To be able to say so much and to say it so calmly, Jack said, puts all our modern efforts to shame. Why should I write a book of five hundred pages when Homer has said everything I want to say in three lines? He called the waiter and paid. Why, he said, is Homer able to say these things with such simplicity and we cannot? Outside it was still drizzling, but more lightly. We went on along the river bank. Compared to Homer *all* writing is sentimental, he said. Even

Chaucer. Even Shakespeare. Much as I love English literature, he said, I have to admit that a strain of sentimentality and unfocussed emotion runs through it. It is not confined to the Victorians. Think of the Monk's Tale of Ugolino eating his children in the locked tower. Think how much more austere Dante's original is than Chaucer's retelling. Think of the murder of MacDuff's children, we are not all that far here from the death of Little Nell. Much as I love English literature, he said, I cannot help feeling that this is a weakness to which it is all too prone. Today, of course, he said, there is nothing but that, cynicism and sentimentality, sentimentality and cynicism, two facets of the same thing. In the winter he wears a Loden coat he bought in Milan and in the summer an old white jacket which is always scrupulously clean or, on exceptionally hot days, shorts and an open shirt. That is what I miss most now I live by myself, he says, the smell and sound of the iron. I love to watch efficiency at work, he says, whether it is a carpenter making a cupboard or a woman ironing a shirt. Why, he says, does that sense of efficiency, of the skill of the hands, seem to be missing when one watches a painter or sculptor at work? That is the most interesting problem of aesthetics, he said as we walked across Hampstead Heath one day last summer. I do not speak of the writer, he said, writing, alas, is as far removed from ironing a shirt or making a cupboard as it is possible to get. When you write every word has to be sought for, every letter even, if your spelling is as shaky as mine. But even the sculptor fails to convey that feeling of well-being which the humblest craftsman or housewife invariably produces. Perhaps, he said, it is because the artist *cares* too much. There must be an element of the mechanical and the repetitive in true craftsmanship, the sense that the hands have done this so often before that they can be trusted to do it again with the brain on hold. That is what gives older art its glory, he said, its glow. And that is the best part of family life. The sound of the cat running down the stairs in the early morning, as he always does, stopping to drink from his bowl, and then the banging of the flap as he hurries out. The sound of people waking up around you and doing what they do every morning, washing, dressing, automatically, instinctively, before they are properly awake. That is why I loathe the sound of the radio first thing in the morning, he said, and why I forbade my children to switch it on. That alien mechanical voice propels you into linear time, he said, and the beauty of the early morning is its repetitiousness, the fact that this morning is like all other mornings. We only value those things, he said, when we have lost them. When you live alone, he said that day on Hampstead Heath, nothing is automatic because everything could always be other than it is, everything is accompanied by thought, by will. Should I get up or stay in bed a little longer? Should I read in bed or get up? Should I have one piece of toast or two? I almost think I got married, he said, because I found a life filled with such meaningless choices deadly and destructive. When you are married, he said, there is no time for such decisions and no need for them either. When two or more people are living together habits form and are maintained and without the web of habit we are likely to fall right through the floor. Kafka is the great poet of solitude, he said, even though he lived with his family for most of his life. That is why he is the representative writer of our century. Solitude, he said, is not a matter of living alone, many of those who lived alone, such as Swift, were not engulfed by solitude. No, he said, it means being cut off from the past and the future, feeling in your bones that you no longer belong as of rights to the family of man. When Kafka says that he has no future and no present and not even a past to direct him, he said, he is saying that he finds himself in a solitude in which everything is possible and nothing is meaningful. When you live alone today, he said, you become aware of the importance of routine and rituals. You lie in bed and you wonder why you should get up. You brush your teeth and you wonder whether to go back over the top row a second time. You open a cupboard and you cannot decide what clothes to wear that day. When you are living with a wife and children, he said, you always feel that there is not

Gabriel Josipovici 55

enough time to think, and you long to have that time, but when you are living alone you realise that not having enough time is a blessing which you have now lost for ever. The greatest joys, he said, as we approached Hampstead Ponds, are those which form the ground of our existence, those of which we are not even aware until we have lost them, and those which come upon us unexpectedly, in the wake of some automatic activity. My best thoughts, he said, always come as I am getting out of my bath in the evening, but they do not come when I have been wracking my brain, they only come when I have been washing myself automatically and drying myself automatically and am about to step automatically into my pyjamas. That is why people do not know what to do with themselves when they retire, he said. That is why so many women who have no need to desperately look for work. We often say, he said, that it is a symptom of the modern unease, this need to be always at work, that it is a way of burying our heads in the sand, a sign of our inability to be with ourselves and at ease. But it may not be exactly that. It may be that people sense that it is only by doing something regular and automatic that they will release the unexpected in their lives. A wise old bird like Wallace Stevens, he said, as we stopped to watch a group of children paddling in the ponds, simply refused to retire. He went on working till the day he died, crossing the park every morning to the insurance office in Hartford where he had worked for most of his life, and crossing it back on his way home every evening. He knew that if he had all day to think about his poetry he would probably not write another line. He knew that it was only by following his regular routine of walking to the office and back every day and forgetting about poetry in the course of every day that he would be able to go on writing. Every morning as he walked to work he would compose some lines of poetry. He would hand these over to his typist when he arrived and keep the typewritten lines she handed back to him in his office drawer. Then as he prepared to go home he would take them out and look at them, put them in his pocket and set off, adding a few lines as he walked back or reworking those already typed. And so the days passed and the poems grew, the result of all those ordinary days in Hartford, Connecticut, USA. When we are tied to an office, he said as we skirted the ponds, we long to be free, but once we are free we find that things aren't exactly as we had imagined them. We had dreamed of writing our memoirs, of spilling the beans on the advertising industry in which we had spent our lives, we even had a title for them, *Malice in Wonderland*, but when we sit down at our desk, at our leisure, a glass of whisky at our side to refresh us, we find that everything seems to evaporate in our heads and even if we manage to grab a memory out of the blue and put it down it looks wooden and clumsy and many thousands of miles from what it was really like. So we get up to refill our glass and sit down again, feeling refreshed, but the same thing happens again. We try jettisoning pen and paper and lying down on the couch, the glass of whisky at our side, and speaking our memoirs into a tape-recorder, but our voice sounds alien and monotonous to us and the whole exercise suddenly seems futile. We dream perhaps of learning a language, he said, Chinese say, or Russian, but the days seem much shorter than we had expected, a few drinks before lunch, a snooze after, a few drinks before and after dinner, a glance at the telly and the day's gone by. And the worst of it is that there is no longer any excuse. Before, when we slaved away to earn our living, we could blame the office and look forward to our retirement, but now we are retired and it isn't any better. What was that thought I so much wanted to put down? What was that memory I knew I needed time to ponder? Well now I have time and it's as far away from me as it ever was. We grow sluggish. We grow bitter. We smoke and drink too much. We try to stop ourselves thinking about the failure of our dream. For now it is clear that it was not the fault of the office. It was us. Our mind is blank. Our heart is cold. Every day death creeps a little closer, the death we fear but also the death we begin to long for because it will put an end to these terrible days of emptiness and hopelessness.

I have trained myself to lead a regular life he said. I get up at exactly the same time every day, I eat at exactly the same time every day, I walk at exactly the same time every day, I write for exactly the same time every day. When despair is in danger of engulfing me, he said, I turn to my Homer or my Kafka or my Dante. But it often happens, he said, that I am aware of how arbitrary such routines are, how easy it would be to let them slide. Nothing, he said, can take the place of the family rush and bustle, the children getting ready for school and the dog having to be taken for his walk. Order, he said as we began to walk up the hill towards Highgate ponds. The regular discipline of the monastery. That is the only way to make life more than a set of reactions to the ticking of the clock. But when you are alone it is never the same thing. We *know* it could be different. We know we do not really need to get up, we know we do not really need to go out walking, we know we do not really need to write. We know, he said, that in the long run it makes no difference whether we sit at our desk and write or whether we don't. But these thoughts must be put out of our minds, he said. We must think short, limit our perspective. To do otherwise is to begin the long slide towards misery and despair. We must remind ourselves how we would feel if we did not sit down and write, did not finish the book we were working on. Everything I have published till now, he said, good and bad, and some of it has been good and some bad, everything I have published has really been in the form of sketches, lightning drawings which capture something, some of them did manage to capture something, but all human beings have one big work in them, think of Virgil, of Rabelais, of Cervantes, of Sterne, of Wordsworth, of Proust, and there comes a point in life when one has to accept that and leave the sketches and the drawings behind. But of course, he said, as we went down again towards Highgate Ponds, when it is time to get up in the morning we are not Virgil or Cervantes or Proust, we are just ourselves with our usual load of confusion and doubt and anxiety and hesitation. And yet the sense of the one great work will not leave one. Regularity, he said. Discipline. The limited perspective. That is essential. Because once you start asking why regularity, why discipline, you very quickly find yourself asking why writing why living and then who knows what might happen? When there is no longer a reason outside yourself for your life to be regular, he said, then discipline starts to look like an absurdity, a perversion. And yet, in spite of everything he said that day by Highgate Ponds, I always wake up in an optimistic frame of mind. When I think about life I am a pessimist, Francis Bacon said to David Sylvester, but I have an optimistic nervous system. I know exactly what he means. And I persist in my absolute belief in the inherent value and worth of artistic making. I persist in believing that the thoughts about meaninglessness and absurdity that I have just been expressing are the promptings of the Devil and, even if they cannot be refuted, must not be listened to. Not, he said, because I necessarily believe in redemption or in the social value of art, but because I believe we each of us, or I at any rate, would be a more unhappy and smaller and meaner person if I was not committed to writing in the way I am. In spite of everything, he said, I hold that regularity and discipline, without which there is no making, are a good which cannot be questioned. We cannot tell what the result will be, he said, we cannot tell if what we make will stand the test of time or not, we cannot tell if the choices we have made are the result of blindness or visions, meanness or generosity, compulsion or grace. But that not being able to tell is *part of what it is all about*. Not 'I believe because it is absurd', but the painful acceptance that there can never be such a thing as certainty in this realm. He suggested we cross over to Highgate cemetery and I followed him as he led the way. Even when a work is done, he said, who is to say that it could not have been put together in some completely different way? I thought it was constructed in the best possible way as I was working on it and perhaps I still do, but who is to say that I'm right? Who is *ever* to say? We can only trust our instinct, he said as we walked up the hill, and hope we have trained it well throughout the course of our lives. Fastidiousness, he said as we turned into Highgate Cemetery. The very word raises a dismissive smile. But why should that be the case? Is it not the culture which smiles so dismissively that needs to be examined? Do we not have to understand the roots of such an attitude? What I am trying to say, Jack said, is that the modern imperative to immerse yourself in the filth and despair of life, the filth and the despair of so much present-day London and New York and Bogota and Rio, the modern insistence that life is to be found down there with the cops and the robbers, the addicts and the bums, the terrorists and the mafiosi, and that to read Raymond Queneau under a tree in Kew Gardens on a summer afternoon is to cut yourself off from reality – this must not go unchallenged. It is nothing but Romantic clap-trap and sentimental nonsense, he said, fuelled by guilt and nostalgia and by a terrible confusion at the heart of our culture. Why is Webern less real than rock? he said, and darted through the tombstones away from the main path. Why is *An Ordinary Evening in New Haven* less real than *The Naked Lunch*? There was a time, he said, when I thought one could write about these things and teach people the truth about them, but there comes a moment when you realise that nobody is listening and that all you can do is to try and live according to your beliefs and let the world go hang. It isn't going to change. Nothing you say or write will change it. But it will change you, he said, and started down a grassy path on either side of which the tombstones were covered with ivy. That is why I so enjoy talking to you, he said. There is a natural sensitivity about you, a natural understanding of these matters, which makes conversation between us possible and proves once again that one cannot generalise about nations and races, there will always be individuals who give the lie to generalisations and statistics. Even Bellow, he said, who has analysed modern individualism and its roots so well, even Bellow, intelligent, witty and immensely well-read though he is, succumbs to the Romantic myth that a gangster is more real than a professor, an abattoir than a library, bourbon than water. Where did it spring from, this view of reality? he said. Is it a Christian thing? A Protestant thing? Or the product of our secular romantic age? Why should suffering be real and well-being not? Why should poverty and deprivation be real and having enough money to do what one wants not? Why should the fist in the face be real and not the wind in the hair? I have no answer to these questions, he said, and a part of me is romantic enough to have a sneaking sympathy for Bellow's views. After all, if we have to choose between *Last Exit to Brookly* and *Harper's Bazaar* the choice is pretty obvious. If we have to choose between Dostoevsky and Galsworthy, he said, we won't have to pause very long. But I have the feeling, he said, that the lines have not been drawn in the right places. What about having to choose between *The Faerie Queene* and *Speak Parrot?* or between *Anna Karenina* and *Pierrot mon ami?* Should we not draw the line rather between the supple and the rigid, the humorous and the humourless, the humanly vulnerable and the smugly self-assured? A person like me, he said, a Sephardic Jew brought up in a cultured and sophisticated community, who lacks any attachment to religion or country, can only look with distaste at the mindless trash that assaults our senses at every moment, the mindless beat of the music of the young, the mindless sentimentality of the musak piped at us in every restaurant and railway station, every shopping mall and dentist's waiting-room. The assault of this numbing music on our ears, he said, is one of the disasters of modern civilisation. It has crept up on us without our being aware of it and now pollutes the silence every bit as much as the noxious chemicals poured out by factories pollute the air, the rivers and the seas. Even so-called intellectuals, he said, cannot bear to remain in a room for more than a second without turning on the radio. People have to have music blaring in their ears, he said, and, if possible, images beamed into their eyes. The idea that you can read a book, he said, put it down, think about what you have just read, pick it up again, or the idea that you can reread a book – such notions, common to civilised people for centuries, are fast disappearing.

We feel ourselves to be a dying breed, he said that day in Highgate Cemetery, we watch as the tide of barbarism rises and we sense that it will soon wash us away. And yet, he said, as we joined the main path again, it would be foolish to give way to despair. Democracy, no doubt, has spread. Advances in medicine have alleviated the sufferings of millions. Who would wish to return to the 1750s or 1850s or even the 1950s? We must live and write as though there were people out there ready to read us as we need to be read, he said, to listen to us as we need to be listened to. We would be in breach of trust if we did not go on writing in the way we feel we should, he said, and saying what we feel should be said. It is vital, he said, not to succumb to the values of society at large, not to be swayed by the siren voices that preach truth and reality to us. We must retain our fastidiousness, he said, and we sat down on the broad slab of Herbert Spencer's tomb and gazed across the path at the toad-like bust of Karl Marx. We must not be put off by the thought that we might appear foolish or prissy or out of touch, he said. As long as our minds are sound, as long as our health lasts, we must go on doing what we know to be right. I do not believe in much, he said, but I believe in this. Not all the time, but most of the time. And it does not of course grow any easier, he said, on the contrary, it grows harder and harder every day, as our energy decreases and the evidence of the world's crassness and philistinism increases and it is clear that nothing we write or say will make any difference. It is easy to be a painter at the age of twenty, Braque said, but quite another at fifty. Those of us who are past fifty, he said, have learned the truth of this only too well. I no longer have any hope that anything will change significantly in the course of my lifetime. I know precisely the quality of my work. I know that it is not very good but not very bad either, perhaps it is good, or good to medium, but at any rate it is incomparably better than most of what is produced today. But why should anybody in this country be interested in what I write? Or why should anybody anywhere be interested, for that matter? More and more, he said, I feel my work slipping between the borders of every country, those black lines on the maps that mark the boundaries. But we must go on in the only way we know, he said, and we got up and approached Marx's tomb and examined the gold lettering on the plinth supporting the hideous bust and turned away. The great hope we had of making the world sit up and listen, he said, that hope begins to fade in one's forties and is clearly no longer to be entertained when we pass fifty. But in any case it was a childish wish, an old atavistic desire for our dreams and those of the world. Perhaps, he said, as we left the cemetery and set off down the Highgate streets to the Heath, the gradual extinction of such hopes is only a sign that we are growing up and learning to accept that this is how things are and have always been. But still, he said, such a gap between our dreams and the world is very hard to live with. We may accept it with our minds but large parts of us go on clinging to the old vision. Perhaps for someone like me, he said, someone with my background and the life I have led, the old vision is stronger than it would be for others, who have been born and grown up in one country and have been able to test themselves against the same reality for the duration of their lives. What he missed, he said, was not a sense of native place, for he felt he could be happy and creative (the two went together) anywhere. No, what he missed, he said was the sense of being taken for granted, the sense of a circle of people around him who had known him since he was a child, had known his parents perhaps since their childhood. He missed being simply the son of his parents, the grandson of his grandparents, and having friends, not necessarily close friends but friends, who were themselves the children and grandchildren of friends of his parents and grandparents. That is the hardest part of being uprooted, he said, that you have to start from scratch each time you meet someone. As if you had to *justify* yourself before each new acquaintance. Not just telling them about yourself if asked, but simply facing them as nothing but yourself. The air between me and others is too thin, he said, it does not have the opacity of whole life stories taken for granted. He said he had only realised what it was he had lost as the years had gone by. As one grows older, he said, one feels more and more isolated if one is not amongst one's own. More and more, he said, he felt the need for a world of relatives and the relatives of relatives, for a world where now, as always, he would have been at home, and flowered, and fulfilled himself. But at the same time, he said, he was well aware of the fact that that was a small and stifling world, a world in which life passed by without any actual achievement, and he knew too, as soon as the feeling came upon him, which it did more and more frequently these days, that it was no use longing for such a world, it would never return, he would never realise it except in his imagination, negatively, as a lack, and he repeated that it was a world in which life was frittered away, in talk and meals and idle gossip, a world in which no-one ever achieved anything, but then nothing was ever achieved by anyone anyway, he said, and all ambition, however noble, was a mirage and an illusion, and his present life of lonely striving in an alien world was even emptier and vainer than it would have been had he grown up as his parents had grown up, in a world of friends and relatives and all the rest of it, and yet even so, he said, he could never quite let go the thought that a solitary life of striving was something after all, and he said that he had only felt himself come alive when he arrived in England, part of it, he said, had to do simply with the weather, a temperate climate like England's was conducive to activity and thought but the heat he had experienced in Egypt, when you lay naked at night with the windows open and sweated onto the sheets and couldn't get to sleep till an almost imperceptible breeze arrived with the dawn, to be quickly dissipated by the rising sun, left him feeling drained and lethargic, but part of it was also due to his fortunate escape at the age of fifteen from this stifling world of comfort and talk and play, the world of well-to-do Sephardic Jewry, though some were newly enriched and others, like his own family, relatively impoverished, so that his mother never knew how to make ends meet and had to go out to work and they were the only European family he knew of who did not have a servant, but it was still a life of leisure, he said, and of a community in which laziness was a way of life, a community, he said, in which memories went back to parents and grandparents and even great-grandparents, and in which the servants of his great-grandparents would sometimes appear, grizzled and distinguished, and be welcomed and talk about old times in the old house and be given a meal and then go to sleep in the garden under the mango and guava trees. All that I miss, he said, though I was hardly aware of it at the time, and although I had already in a sense experienced it as something missing in my first years as a child in France with my mother trying to escape from the Germans during the war. The lack of all that, nevertheless, he said, as we crossed the Heath back towards Hampstead Ponds, is something I feel more and more as I grow older, like a leg that has been amputated and yet is still capable of giving you pain. There is no cushion for someone like me, he said, no cushion in custom or tradition or a common past, each day is a new day and each encounter has to start from the beginning. On the other hand, he said, he had been fortunate to have escaped when he did from that other world, a world which anyway, after Suez, no longer existed but had been dispersed, to Rome and Paris and Montreal and even London. But I have always avoided the Jewish Egyptian exiles here, he said, they no longer make sense away from their natural habitat and there are too few of them to form a proper immigrant community, only a few old ladies drinking coffee in Pembridge Gardens and Kensington Church Road and lamenting the loss of their wealth and their youth. These were not people he had ever had much in common with anyway, he said, the war years of his earliest childhood had already made an exile of him even when he was amongst them. Perhaps if we are to achieve anything, he said, we need to feel the pain of severing ourselves from such worlds, though it is not a pain that ever decreases or shows signs of disappearing. There are times, he said, when the separation seems to render all one's strivings null from the beginning. That is why Kafka means so much to me, he said, as he means so much to so many people, and why Eliot does too, though this would surprise the English, who have never understood him. For a Jew like myself, he said, even the term exile is a misnomer. I will never have the relationship to Egypt, in which I spent my childhood and part of my adolescence, or to France, where I was born, that Stravinsky and Nabokov had to Russia, for example, he said, since neither was my country in the sense that Russia was theirs. One of my great-grandfathers came from Italy, he said, and another from Rumania, while my mother's father came from Odessa. Egypt was simply the country in which they settled because life there was easy for foreigners and the climate was benign and the people were not inimical to Jews, particularly if they had money. But I have no attachment to the land or the weather of that country, he said, in fact it is a land and a climate which depress and debilitate me, although there are certain aspects of it I sometimes recall with joy and nostalgia, such as the flame trees lining the streets and the early mornings in the desert. It is not the country I miss, he said, but that sense of belonging which I've been trying to express, a sense of living in a world one would only partly understand because one was entering it at a late stage, but that this did not matter, this too was part of what one was, someone who entered late and had of necessity to take much for granted. Whereas in England, he said, I constantly feel the need to understand and be understood, there are no grey areas where trust and tradition can take the slack. Someone like you, he said, though you have little in common with your parents and those with whom you grew up, can still nevertheless see them and know you will be accepted and taken for granted by them. So much of the culture in which I grew up was embarrassingly superficial, he said, but the point is that none of that matters, what matters is simply that this was the environment in which I grew up and suddenly it is gone as though it had never been. What have I in common with the English, he said, or with English Jews? In many ways I feel much further from the latter than I do from some of the former, those old-fashioned cultured English men and women who have at least read the same books as I have and whose values are in some ways so similar to mine, yet there always comes a point, even with the most cultured of them, when I feel like an exotic animal or worse, when I feel that they are placing me in a pigeon-hole, a category, simply because the world from which I come has never impinged upon their own. There are exceptions, of course, he said, both among the English and among the Jews of England, there are always exceptions, thank God, but that is the general sense I get. I have been bred, he said, as though with the exclusive aim of rendering me unfit to be a member of any group or community, for the world to which I feel I belong has vanished and I can only try and carry its virtues within me and to make them work for me in my life. That is not only not an easy task, he said, it is an impossible and self-contradictory task, for no-one can carry the virtues of a community within himself. Moreover, he said, I have to acknowledge that escaping from it when I did was probably the greatest single stroke of good fortune I have had in this life, if you do not count escaping from the Germans with my mother when I was a child and too young really to grasp what was going on. The day I set foot in England, he said, I began to come alive. It was the thirteenth of September 1956 and apparently it was the first fine summer's day that year. From that day on, he said, I began to recognise the value of not belonging, I began to flourish and to feel myself expanding, discovering what I could do. Some of it can be ascribed to the climate, he said, to the cold of the winters which sharpens the senses and fills you with energy, and to the constantly changing skies which make not only each day but each moment of each day different from all the others, instead of the exhausting heat of Egypt and the uniform blue skies of that country. When I came here at the age of fifteen, he said, I began to eat with an appetite I had never known as a child. I found myself actually looking forward to my meals and my mouth would literally water as I stood in line to receive my bun at eleven in the school hall and as I toiled home up the hill on my bicycle I would be thinking with mounting anticipation of the toast I would have for tea. It was the heyday of Horlicks, he said, and a cup of Horlicks before going to bed not only ensured that one slept like a baby, but that one went on putting on weight, so that in no time at all I had changed from a skinny child to a plumpish adolescent. Horlicks and Bovril, he said, that was the taste of the England I came to in 1956. It was the taste of an England I thought I could come to know and love, he said, it went with the dry-stone walling of the Cotswolds in which I first lived, and with the woods and streams which evoked in me feelings I had never experienced in the desert in Egypt. But the longer I live here, he said, the less I understand the country or its inhabitants. I still love the changing skies, he said, and the countryside, both in the south and in the north, and would not exchange them for any others, but the ethos of the country itself is another matter, the values I see people holding on to, whether they are rich or poor, the smugness, the indifference, the inarticulateness, the terrible sense of lack of hope and lack of direction, the only god worshipped the god of money. Money money money. Nevertheless, he said, one of the reasons I am so fond of you is that you are the only friend I have, or perhaps I should say the only English friend, who does not constantly complain about the English and England and does not go on and on about wishing to live elsewhere. If only my other friends understood the pain it gives me, he said, to hear them grumbling about England and constantly voicing their desire to be elsewhere, they would perhaps refrain in my presence. But they have not the imagination to understand how I might feel, he said, and so they no sooner see me than they begin their interminable whinings, their interminable grumblings, and they no sooner see me than they hurry to tell me how ill at ease they feel here and how they cannot wait till the next holiday they are to take abroad or the plans they have to emigrate to America or Australia or Italy or Cyprus, as though these places were any better, but for them they are better or they think they are better because they were not born there and did not grow up there and were not educated there and because, unlike me, they have nothing but hatred and revulsion for the communities in which they did grow up and for their families and relations and the friends of their youth and their schooling and everything else connected with their childhood and adolescence. I have never met any people which had such a hatred of its childhood and such a distaste for its past and such a lack of enthusiasm for its future as this one, he said. It is as though the old myths of God and of Empire had died quite suddenly, from one day to the next, and there was nothing there to take their place. What ideals there are in this society, he said, are imported from America, and are no more than the ideals of a soft-hearted illiterate teenage girl. But these are the ideals embraced by every sector of the population, he said, so eager are they to forget their childhood and schooling and adolescence and their families and the towns they grew up in. To hear most of my friends talk, he said as we came in sight of Hampstead Ponds again, you would say that they had never experienced a happy day in the whole of their childhood, that it was misery and narrowness and meanness from beginning to end. Even the well-off, he said, those who have been to public schools and had everything they could ask for, have made a habit of grumbling about the philistinism and sadism of these institutions and about how it has destroyed them and left them cold and unfeeling and suspicious and with the perpetual sense of being rejected by their families and un-loved and perpetually wounded in the very core of their be-ings. Whereas my childhood, he said, despite the fear and insecurity and uncertainty, was extraordinarily happy, extra-ordinarily rich and full and interesting, for which no doubt I have to thank my mother and what she gave me in terms of security and self-confidence and what she taught me by example about resourcefulness and the deep pleasures that come from making do with the little one has and from doing well that for which one has a gift. We cannot achieve very much unless we love ourselves, he said, and we cannot love ourselves unless our parents have loved us. That is why, he said, in spite of everything, I am an optimist. If, like Bacon, I have an optimistic nervous system, he said, I must owe that to the unstinting love my mother gave me and the trust I had in her. I am helped of course by the authors I treasure, he said, Proust and Dante and Wallace Stevens and the rest. When my friends depress me by telling me how much they despise England and the English, he said, how they loathe the meanness and greyness and lack of joy they see all round them, how their hearts expand as soon as they set foot on foreign soil and contract again into little tight knots as soon as they arrive back home, when they go on about how expensive and foul the hotels are here and how deep rooted and destructive the class system is, how desperate the plight of the hospitals, how the public libraries, once the jewel in the crown of every town and village, are now practically without books and even those there are are housed in buildings that grow dingier by the hour, buildings stacked with computers and retrieval systems and cassettes and videos but hardly a single new book, when they depress me in this way, he said, by pouring their misery and anger and despair all over me, then I can turn away and bury myself in my beloved Kafka, in my beloved Eliot, in my beloved Sterne. One would have thought they took a perverse pleasure in tormenting me in this fashion, he said, I who have chosen England and have made my home in England and am too old to move now even if I wanted to or could think of anywhere to move to. For the thinking man, he said, everywhere is equally bad, the failures and injustices equally conspicuous, though no doubt there are different kinds of failure, different kinds of injustices in France and Italy and Germany, in Canada and Australia and Cyprus. The writers and pundits in those countries are no less quick than they are in this country, he said, to point out the injustices and the failures of their respective countries, but you do not find the inhabitants moaning about their lot or talking of nothing but their desire to emigrate or at least to go on longer and longer holidays and return less and less frequently, and for shorter and shorter periods, but in England this is just what you are always hearing. The world is all one today, he said, and there is nowhere to escape to. Radio and television have ruined us, he said, it would be quite unnatural of course to shut our ears and eyes to them and yet it is equally unnatural to try and cope morally and psychologically with the horrors they report day after day and week after week. If we respond to them as we should, as human beings, and try to do something about them, then they will swallow us and our savings in a matter of months, but if we do what we have to do in order to survive, that is harden our hearts, then we have to live with these hardened hearts and that is not good for us or for those who come into contact with us. There is no way out of the dilemma, he said as we left the Heath, we cannot shut our ears and we cannot open our hearts, we have created things to which our organs have not had a chance to adapt. I have tried going for months without listening to the news, without seeing the news, without reading a paper, but the effort is too great, one feels that one is holding something at bay and no life can be lived like that, day after day, week after week. On the other hand, he said, when one listens and sees one is forced to protect oneself, one has to hold the reports of famine and repression, of violence and injustice at a distance, treat them as stories in which one is not required to believe, to register them and yet not register them, but it takes its toll, it takes its toll. To be frank, he said, I am sometimes greatly relieved by the thought that I will soon be dead and no longer have to go on with this psychological juggling act, day after day, registering and not registering, taking in and not taking in, knowing and not knowing. Not tomorrow, probably, but in not too long a time, five or ten or even twenty years, it is the thought that it will eventually come to an end which is such a relief, he said as we reached the bus-stop on Rosslyn Hill. Someone like myself, he said, whose life has in a sense always been split, should be able to cope with it better than most, but perhaps the opposite pertains, the fact that my life has always been split only makes me more aware of this and more vulnerable to it. A name like mine, he said, stepping out into the road to see if a bus was in sight, a name like mine is a sign and index of the split. Why Toledano? Because, no doubt, my family came from Toledo at the time of the expulsion from Spain. It is a name, he said, of which we have always been proud, and the given names of my ancestors reflect this, Baruch the blessed one, Abraham after the first patriarch, Isaac after his son, David, Daniel, Moses, one could reconstruct the whole Bible and the whole of Jewish history from the given names of my family, he said, but what name have I been given? Jack. Jacques, actually, in the French style, but here in England, Jack, as my great-uncles were called Victor and Henri and, yes, wait for it, Napoleon. By comparison with Napoleon, he said, Jack is a relatively harmless name, nevertheless, for anyone with ears to hear the combination of Jack and Toledano is more than an anomaly or even a lapse of taste, it is a symbol. Jack and the Beanstalk, fine, he said, Jack and Jill ditto, but Jack the Jew, exiled from Toledo five hundred years ago, that is something to chew over. But it is the name my parents gave me, he said, looking at his watch and once more stepping out into the road to see if the bus was on its way, and it is the name I have to live with. Of course, he said, I could change my name to Toll or Tilden, an aficionado of the game of tennis like me, he said, would find it a source of pride to carry the name of Tilden, but I cannot do it, he said, it goes against the grain. On the other hand, he said, I could ignore the Jack and return to the name of great-grandfather, Moses, or of my great-great-grandfather, Jacob, after all, I have known girls change their name from Susan to Shoshana and from Phoebe to Miriam, but I cannot do it, it would imply an assertion of Jewishness of which I do not feel myself capable, for, he said, I feel myself as far from this Moses and this Jacob as I do from the original Moses and Jacob, and almost as far as I do from Jill's Jack and Beanstalk Jack. So I have to live with this hybrid, he said, this sphinx or centaur, it is a symbol of all the discontinuities which go to make up my life and I would have to feel that I could mend or heal them in that life before I could venture to change the name, but where would I find the means for such a healing? I can only live the anomaly, he said, and accept it as a part of what is given. Acceptance, he said as we walked one afternoon from Putney to Barnes along the river, acceptance is a word nobody understands any more and nobody wants to understand. We feel, he said, that if things are bad they ought to be changed and if they cannot be changed then it is either our fault or, more usually, the fault of someone else or of the state or the system or some equally abstract entity. If we could understand, he said, how it is possible to curse the misfortune that has lighted upon us and at the same time to accept it, we would not only be more human, we would also be much happier. But for us, today, he said as we passed the boat-houses, the word acceptance stinks of passivity, we have no understanding, he said, of how it is possible to accept in an active and positive way. The Greeks understood this, he said, and the ancient Hebrews. They knew how it was possible to complain of what Zeus or Poseidon or Jahweh had done to them, even to curse Zeus or Poseidon or Jahweh, and yet at the same time to accept what had befallen them. Much-enduring Odysseus, he said, not only an Odysseus who has suffered much but one who is prepared to swallow many insults, to endure without complaint much hardship in order to gain his long-term objectives. Suffering and enduring have a positive connotation here, he said, they imply self-control and self-belief as well as belief in the ultimate benevolence of the Gods. But then the *Odyssey* is a comedy, which means that for the protagonists everything will turn out well in the end. What befalls the protagonists of Greek tragedy, he said, is usually far far worse than they or their audience could have envisaged even in their wildest nightmares. Think of Oedipus, of Pentheus, of Hercules, Hecuba, Agamemnon. Think of Job. How to curse God, he said, and yet go on talking to Him, that is the secret of the ancient Greeks and Hebrews. Our curses today are all inward, he said, they are too feeble even to reach the outside world. We pity the victims of tyranny and oppression, he said, and we pity ourselves as the victims of ill-luck or the machinations of others. Our inability to curse properly is one with our inability to experience our lives as in any sense destined, which means in effect to experience our lives as having solidity. He went on to say that Kierkegaard understood this well and that in his lecture or essay on the difference between Greek and modern tragedy in *Either/Or* he had probed more deeply than anyone before or since into the weaknesses, even contradictions, of the modern condition. Auden once wrote a clerihew on Kierkegaard, he said, which demonstrates perfectly that light verse can be profound, in the right hands: Sören Kierkegaard/ Tried very hard/ To take the leap/ But fell in a heap. That is exactly right, he said, though I gather a Dane would object to the rhyming of Kierkegaard with hard. I believe, he said, it rhymes instead with whore. Like all the greatest Romantics, he said, Kierkegaard was filled with Romantic longing and at the same time deeply critical of it, he was caught in the trap of Romantic nostalgia and yet could see clearly where it would lead. Like Lichtenberg and Kleist, he said, he intuited what was wrong with the whole Enlightenment project, how much had been lost in the course of the seventeenth and eighteenth centuries, but he could only gesture towards this, not make it the basis for any ethic or metaphysic. The Greeks *suffered*, we *sorrow*, Kierkegaard said in that essay. He did not mean that the Greeks were blessed in their suffering but that Greek tragedy shows us men and women who, whatever blows have fallen upon them, manage nevertheless to find the words to speak their grief, reviling the gods and lamenting the fact that they have ever been born. All that is closed to Kierkegaard, he said, and to us. He knows that we have lost the capacity to curse and to bless, though we still feel the need to utter curses and to receive blessing. It is like a hunger that cannot be assuaged, he said, however much you eat. Or perhaps like a hunger of which we are hardly aware but which will not let us alone. That is what creative work can do, he said, it can bring us in touch with our hunger if not assuage it. Creative work, he said, and the work of healing. Doctors are the saints of the modern world, he said, and like the saints of old they do not even know it. The doctor and the composer, he said, are examples of absolute generosity of spirit, absolute selflessness. What they do has nothing to do with the self, and because that is the case blessing sometimes touches them. We writers on the other hand, he said, are deeply contaminated. It is rare, he said, that we can work in such a way that we leave ourselves behind, that we become totally absorbed in the act of making. But that is the only condition in which blessing can touch us. Sportsmen have it to a certain extent, he said, but the goal is too clearly defined there and the desire to win inevitably too prominent. Several weeks sometimes go by without a word from him, but when he fixes a rendezvous he is always there. There is, he says, only a limited amount of time he can sit at his desk and the rest of the time he has to find a way to keep himself amused. There are weeks and even months, he says, when what he needs is total quiet and privacy, and there are weeks and even months when what he needs above all else is company. As one grows older, he says, one does not get better at one's work, only at knowing what will help and what will hinder it. One learns what to avoid and what to seek, when to push and when to lay off. Though of course one does not always get it right, even after a life-time. There are days when one thinks what one needs is total solitude and one quickly discovers that one's thoughts are just going round and round in one's head and that one is getting more and more exhausted simply doing nothing, until one gets in such a state that only the sound of a friendly voice can help, and there are days when one thinks one needs to walk and talk but as soon as one has set out on a walk with a friend one realises that what one really needed was solitude and silence. There are days, he says, when one goes into an art gallery convinced that there one will find the peace and quiet of mind that will lead to the breakthrough one has been seek-ing, only to find that it is too hot or too cold or too crowded or that one's shoes hurt or one's head aches and one cannot see the pictures in front of one and even if one can see them one doesn't have the serenity of spirit to take them in, so that one is left wondering why one ever went in the first place and what one ever saw in pictures. It is the same with music. There are days when one goes to a concert, convinced that a certain piece of music is going to make all the difference only to find, once one has settled into one's seat, that one cannot concentrate on the music but is distracted by the elbow of one's neighbour or the hair of the person in front or the heat of the hall or else one's mind keeps drifting to what one has just eaten or done or failed to do and what has to be done the next day and so on and so forth. But there are days too, he says, when one comes into a concert feeling disgruntled and unwell, with one's heart pounding and one's mind racing and one settles down convinced that one has made a mistake, that one should never have gone out, or, if one had, not to a concert, that going to a concert was really the last thing one should have done. And yet the music only has to begin and suddenly everything that has been troubling one drops away and one enters the music and lives the music and travels with the music and enters that magic land where doors that had long been closed open of their own accord and the deepest and darkest things become clear and comprehensible and, if not livable-with, at least recognised and accepted. The most complete musical experience of my life, he said, came with a performance not of Bach or Beethoven or even Mozart but when I first heard Harrison Birtwistle's *Triumph of Time*. I seem to remember there was a Mozart overture to begin with, he said as we stopped to watch a flight of geese, and I was sitting in the top tier at the Festival Hall, which is a horrible place to be but those were the only tickets I could afford in those days. I had done too much during the day and found myself sitting there trying to concentrate on the Mozart and feeling it was going to be one of those evenings in the concert hall that are a complete and utter waste of time and money. The orchestra was too far away, the ceiling was oppressively close, the music tinkled on, utterly meaningless, and came to a stop and people applauded. I thought of leaving there and then but I was in the middle of a row and anyway the conductor was returning for the Birtwistle. I closed my eyes and the music started. Suddenly everything changed. I found myself living within that pulse and feeling it as a beat that could have been a fraction of a second or a thousand years and I knew that it was both, and that art was not about beauty or sadness but about truth, and as the great procession moved forward and the brass and woodwind flashed out and then retreated again into the low rumble of the march I felt myself in touch with that which was most basic and essential in the universe and discovered that it was one with what was most basic and essential in myself. My mind was strangely detached and I found myself wondering why these essential truths had always seemed so elusive, since there they were, quite concrete, parading before me, but I knew too that as soon as the music ended they would vanish again. But by and large, he said, as one grows older one does get to know oneself a little better, at least in this respect, and when one opts for solitude and silence it usually means that solitude and silence are what one needs, and when one opts for company it is because only company will help. We were passing in front of Harrod's Depositary. One has to make the city work for one, he said, or one will be crushed by it. One has to know where to walk and when to stay at home. Too many people, he said, are utterly crushed and destroyed by cities as they are utterly crushed and destroyed by the country. They rush about when they should be sitting still and they stay indoors when they should be taking advantage of the fine weather. That is where a family and its routines is so important, he said, it acts as a buffer against the destruction of the soul, both in the city and in the country, even though, at the same time, it stops one from ever responding as fully as one might to the city and the country. As long as I was married, he said, I was protected against the depths of despair, although by the same token I was debarred from the heights of joy. I could never say that

I have no regrets, he said, and I do not believe people who say they have no regrets. But what good is it to look back and wonder if things might have been different? When one is embedded in family life, he said, one is cushioned against the world. Perhaps, he said, it is because I never believed it would last that it did not last. Because it always seemed to me that I was *playing* at being a husband and father and that my wife and children were *playing* at being my wife and children, he said as we passed under Hammersmith Bridge, and that sooner or later the game would be over and we would all go our separate ways. So he was not really surprised, he said, when it came to an end. I would like to think, he said, that I have done my best work since I have been alone, but I am not sure that that is true. The fact of the matter, he said, is that one works as well as one can for as long as one can, and if one is lucky then grace descends every so often, though nothing can tell you in advance, of course, that this is the time. These things do not bear close scrutiny, he said as we stood aside to let a group of cyclists go by. One can only work in the dark to the best of one's ability and trust that if it has happened once it will happen again. But there is no saying that it will. We have pushed against all the doors, Proust writes in *Contre Sainte-Beuve,* he said, and not one of them has yielded, and then, when we have quite given up and resigned ourselves to the doors staying shut for ever one of them suddenly opens and we are through. I remember marking that passage in pencil when I was seventeen, he said, and reading it aloud to my best friend in Oxford, I remember copying it out in my notebook and recopying it in every subsequent notebook I bought, but now I have to say that I think it is overly romantic and optimistic. That door may never open, he said. There may not be a door. Or it may open just when one has nodded off for a few seconds. And yet, he said, increasing his pace so that I had difficulty keeping up with him, we must not grow cynical, that is the sin against the Holy Ghost and that is the sin committed by so-called post modernism in all its manifestations. Doors and windows do open, he said, anyone who has taken part in sports and anyone who has practised an art knows that there are sudden inexplicable advances, that things do fall into place, that the whole is occasionally more than the sum of its parts. But we should not try to understand how or why, he said, we should simply convince ourselves that this is how things are. That was one thing I had against my wife, he said, she was bitten by the modern need to *understand*, as though understanding would solve everything. When I met her, he said, she was seeing an analyst, and when we parted she was seeing an analyst. I do not know if it was the same one. I can say this to you, he said, because I know we share the same views about psychoanalysts and psychoanalysis, but there are not many people one could talk to today who would agree with us. Yet mankind has got along perfectly well for centuries without psychiatrists and psychoanalysts and counsellors and guides, he said, and today when such people are thick on the ground and practically everyone you meet is either seeing one of them or training to be one of them or actually is one of them, people are no happier or better able to do the things they have to do than they ever were. When I talk to these people, he said, or to people who regularly consult these people, I feel as though I had stepped onto a foreign planet and the people I am talking to only appear to be like me in the way they look and in the language they use, but in reality they are a totally foreign species, with whom I have nothing in common and will never have anything in common. It is the same with priests and the people who consult priests, he said, they can be interesting and charming but we belong to different worlds. Except perhaps for Anglican priests, he said, because they are not priests at all but merely rather sad and thoughtful ordinary people. When we got married, he said, my wife assured me that she would never again have any need to consult an analyst but only a year or two later she was at it again, and though I asked her to explain to me why she was doing it she was totally unable to do so, except to say that she needed to speak to someone who was neither a relative nor a friend if she was to understand herself. I do not know where this mania for understanding oneself has come from he said, but it clearly exerts a powerful hold on people, and I do not know why she could not talk to someone in a park or on a bus if it was a stranger she wanted to talk to, it would have been cheaper, but perhaps she was afraid. When I asked her why she wanted to understand herself and if she thought such a thing was possible she turned on me and told me I always tried to crush her. But I was only telling her the truth, he said, there is no such thing as understanding without suffering. Money is no substitute. At Barnes Bridge we turned up Barnes High Street and emerged at the pond, which was deserted except for a woman sitting on a bench with four dogs at her feet. I have passed my life among domestic animals, he said, first dogs and then cats and then dogs again and now my cat. There is nothing like animals for reminding one of the basic elements of life, he said. There is nothing more joyful for a father than seeing his children rolling on the ground with the family dog or sitting with the family cats on their laps. Teach children to love and respect animals, he said and you have taught them the essentials of a happy and dignified life. But what can you do? he said. They grow up and they turn into strangers, with the tastes of strangers and the attitudes of strangers. Music which you loathe and despise they go around listening to all day. Food you have taken care never to feed them they stuff themselves with all day. And no sooner have they reached the age of puberty than they start going around with girlfriends and boyfriends the very sight of whom makes you feel ill and whose accents and appearance you would have thought would be as offensive to their ears and eyes as they are to yours. But not a bit of it. These are people they are prepared to touch and to kiss and sooner or later to sleep with. And what can you do? The spirit of the times has got to them in spite of all your efforts and it is as much as you can do to remember that they are indeed your children. Biological links, he said, and we left the pond behind and followed a path over a little bridge into Barnes Common, cannot be said to be links at all. I can see my wife's ears in my youngest child and my mother's eyes in the eldest, but that makes it all the more uncanny because they have nothing of my wife and mother except for these ghostly remnants. Perhaps, he said, bending down to pat a dog that had appeared in front of us out of nowhere, I have been a bad father, but what can you do when you feel more and more like a stranger and an actor as the years pass by? The dog's owner crossed our path and gave us a dirty look. Perhaps, Jack said, I only married in order to root myself in this country, but all it did was make me realise how much of a stranger I would always be. That is what living does for you, he said, it teaches you bit by bit who and what you really are. Psychiatrists can't do it, he said, and psychoanalysts can't do it, only life with its repeated unexpected blows can do it. Bit by bit. Blow by blow. We were walking through the old cemetery with its creeper-covered tombstones and monuments and its derelict paths. I began to write, he said, to clean out my head. Not because I had 'anything to say' and not because I wanted to make beautiful objects or tell beautiful stories but quite simply to clean out my head and stop myself going mad. Rather like the young Swift, he said, who tells us in an early letter that his mind was 'like a conjured spirit, that would do mischief if I would not give it employment'. Literary critics and reviewers, he said, can never understand this. For them a good novel espouses ideas or reveals what they call the depths of human suffering or transports them into magic lands. I am not interested in baring my breast, he said, or in shouting out loud that I believe in freedom from oppression and don't approve of torture. But I am not interested either in sticking wings and tails on my characters and letting them give free rein to their desires. There is nothing more depressing than free reins, he said. I write in order to escape the imagination, not to indulge it. That is why I call myself a realist. That is why I *am* a realist. But nowadays realism means endless descriptions of New York brothels or London's underworld, or else it means setting your work in Neasden or Bromley. Unless you are describing a thousand years of Fenland history or a thousand years of West Country history, indirectly, of course, indirectly, but the indirect approach to the old broad sweep is one of the approaches most popular with reviewers at present. It is with this, I am told, that they identify most of all, whatever that means. Of course, he said, there is no reason why anyone but I should be interested in how and why I clean out my head or give my conjured spirit a bit of employment, and yet there is something in human beings that makes them long desperately to be understood and applauded. Understanding by itself is something, but understanding and applause are what we are really all after. And I am no exception of course. It is as though with each new book I had hoped to awake an echo out there in the world and of course I was disappointed when this did not happen and of course I had to work hard at myself to get back on course and go on with my work without paying any attention to the lack of response. As I grow older, he said, and stopped to examine a tombstone, it naturally gets harder and takes longer. When you are young, he said, you can brush off the indifference of the world, confident that it is a temporary mistake that will soon be rectified, or else you imagine that you can survive perfectly well on your own and have no need of the world. But as you grow older, he said as we left the cemetery and crossed one of the many little paths that bisect the Common at this point, you begin to realise that things are not going to change, not in your lifetime at any rate, and you also find it more and more difficult to go on with what seems during most of the hours of the day and night to be a pointless and self-indulgent mode of life, devoted to a pointless and self-indulgent set of activities. That is where discipline is so important, he said, that is where even a tiny crack in the discipline could lead to disaster, though submitting to a meaningless and utterly pointless discipline also seems to be a disaster, and that is where my natural optimism is so crucial, for without it even my iron discipline would soon crack and who knows how it would all end? To give up now would be an unmitigated disaster, he said, it would mean a victory for those who sought to kill me and those like me in the war. My survival, he said, and the production of work, the best work that I can do, is what I owe to whatever forces kept me alive at that time. Of course, he said, to keep going simply for the sake of keeping going may be a different kind of betrayal, but that does not bear thinking about, what is important is that it may just be something else, and it is that something else which we have to keep before us all the time, at all costs. I have often wondered, he said, a few large drops of rain were falling, I have often wondered which is the more dignified, to stop once and for all or to keep going in spite of everything. The one action is in danger of eliciting pity, he said, the other laughter. Which would you rather elicit if you had the choice? I imagine the latter, he said, for the person who elicits laughter is always clothed in a haze of ambiguity, one never knows how far he is conscious of the effect he is producing, how far he *wants* to produce that effect, and how far he is unconscious of the effect he is producing. As Falstaff well knew, he said, who said of himself that he was not only witty in himself but the cause that wit is in other men, and seemed proud of it. But even laughter, he said, now seems to be beyond the reach of so-called literary critics and reviewers. They are driven by the fires of their own righteousness and by the lust to know and understand, to make and unmake, and laughter is of course irrelevant in such circumstances. I could not go on teaching in such a climate, he said, I could not try to reach young people who had been poisoned by my colleagues to such an extent that they had forgotten the meaning of laughter. I could not be part of an institution which was driven by this humourless passion for truth and by an equally humourless morality and where the ability to use language, whether on the part of writers they were studying or of the students themselves was not even considered. They would not have known what good writing was even if they had read it, he said, and there was little chance of that. They will never understand what every artist until today has known, that the omission of a comma or the clumsy repetition of a word within one sentence were indexes of a failure of vision and morality. For a long time, he said, I tried to go my own way and to teach them the values I myself believed in, but there comes a point when you realise you cannot win the war. You may win a skirmish here or even a battle there, but you cannot win the war. In the interests of sanity, he said, it is better to get out then, before you are ground into powder by the unthinking unseeing unfeeling forces ranged against you. The rain had become quite heavy now and he quickened his pace. I became a teacher partly to earn my living, he said, and partly because I believed that it was possible to foster in others the love of good writing I had inherited from my mother and from my teachers, both at school and at Oxford, and most of all of course from the authors I loved. When the first was no longer a problem, he said, and the second was proving more and more of an illusion, it was time to get out. Not that I do not occasionally miss the teaching, he said as we crossed a little bridge over a stream and took a lane that led behind tall buildings on our right and with playing fields on our left, and not that I do not mourn daily the fate of students of literature, now delivered over into the hands of the barbarians and the puritans, but there is such a thing as self-immolation and there is such a thing as self-preservation. Perhaps I was wrong, he said, perhaps as a teacher I was able to do a little good for others at no great personal cost, whereas now I don't even have the satisfaction of that. The way I prefer to look at it, he said as we found ourselves once more by the river, is that I was fortunate to have had a job for half a lifetime which was not demeaning and which allowed me to do and say some of the things which I felt needed to be done and said. I could not have found a job like that thirty years earlier, he said, and I would not be able to find a job like that today. So from a certain point of view I was the most fortunate of men, I did more or less what I wanted and I felt that it had a certain value and I got paid for it. That is a rare enough thing at any time, he said as we once again drew level with the boathouses. In that building, he said, pointing as we walked on towards

Putney Bridge, lived J.R. Ackerley, one of the best English writers of this century and one of the most curious and interesting of men, though probably more to the readers of his books than to his friends and acquaintances for by all accounts he was a maddening person to know. If you want to understand the English homosexual of a certain period, he said, you would do better to read Ackerley than to read Wilde, and if you want to understand modern man's relation to domestic animals you would do better to read Ackerley than to read Gavin Maxwell. His posthumous book of memoirs, *My Father and Myself*, he said, as we approached the building, is far superior to Goethe's *Dichtung und Warheit* and Stendhal's *de l'Amour*, and a lot more fun to read than either. I like the idea, he said as we went into the Star and Garter for a drink and to get out of the rain, of Ackerley's father living peaceably with his family in Richmond and having another family, with whom he presumably lived an equally peaceable life, in Wimbledon. But then if you are a Banana King, as Ackerley senior was, you can presumably get away with such things, and the occasional frolic with a guardsman too. And I love the little bombs he lays along the way, he said as we settled into seats by the window looking down over the river, such as his remark to the reader that 'when you read this I shall be lying under another sod'. That, he said, is worthy of Donne, though a little more daring. Nietzsche maintained, he said, that there were only two German books worth preserving, Goethe's *Conversations with Eckermann* and Lichtenberg's *Fragments*. I personally cannot see what he found in Goethe, unless it was the unintentional humour of a man who took himself wholly seriously and never once, throughout his life, had the slightest inkling of what a smug and pompous figure he cut, though he was no doubt a very brilliant and wise man as well and a very fine poet, but who would quarrel with Nietzsche about Lichtenberg? His *Fragments* is one of the great books of the world, he said, and it is a book I return to with the greatest pleasure, again and again. People talk of Montaigne giving us a sense of what it is like to be an ordinary human being, curious, tolerant and confused. They claim that Montaigne was the first to escape from the deadening hand of rhetoric. I have tried to read Montaigne many times, he said, not least because he was the favourite author of so many writers I admire and respect, such as Gide and Butor and Bernhard, but I have to confess that though there are some nice turns of phrase here and there and one or two very moving passages, what I find in Montaigne is rather the *idea* of the individual than any true sense of a unique person. In the end, he said, returning to the table with our drinks, Montaigne is as full of clichés as Erasmus and Thomas More. It is an unfortunate fact, he said, that the men of that time could only see the world through the prism of Roman literature, and though we may admire their reading, their industry and above all their general decency, they leave us cold, as Roman literature leaves us cold. It is Lichtenberg, he said, who is the true original, the person who catches better than anyone else before Proust the oddity and singularity of human life and how much more *awkward* and varied it is than the schemes and patterns of the philosophers. How clever of the deity, Lichtenberg once remarked, to cut a hole in a cat's face exactly the size of his eyes. Elsewhere he notes the surprise with which he greets, every morning, the sight of his two slippers lying next to each other on the floor beside his bed. Many of his lines, he said, can stand comparison with Chandler's 'I went home and listened to Khachaturian murdering his wife. He called it a violin concerto.' It is worth while to have been alive, he said, as we looked out at the river, now almost hidden by the rain, simply to have been given the chance to read a sentence like that. And Lichtenberg is full of them. What two books would you wish to preserve from the corpus of English literature? he said, and finished his drink and put the glass down on the table again. I mean literature in the English language of course, not literature written exclusively by the English. The poems of Skelton and Hogg's *Diary of a Justified Sinner*? Or the poems of Donne and *Tristram Shandy*? Perhaps we should make it five, he said, not two, for English literature, after all, is immeasurably richer than German. That would allow us to add the poems of Eliot and Stevens and an omnibus volume of Raymond Chandler. I wonder, he said, where Chandler thought up his one-liners? Did he work at them like Flaubert or did they come to him ready-made in the bath? It would be interesting, he said, to examine the influence of Dulwich College on modern English letters, since that remarkable school gave us not only Chandler but that other expatriate Englishman and consummate manipulator of the English language, P. G. Wodehouse. When I think of those two great writers, he said, I wonder what I am doing myself trying to write. I do not know why I started and I do not know why I go on. I only know that I feel much worse when I am not writing than when I am. And sometimes I think, he said, that my role is to demonstrate what happens when one has the need to write but not the talent or the learning or the experience, when one is bereft of ability but the need will not subside. For that in itself is after all interesting and no doubt a condition which, if not general and universal, is at least not peculiar to me. Otherwise there would not be such a rage for creative writing classes and poetry competitions and summer writing courses and the rest of it. But no-one has really addressed this condition, he said, everybody who takes part in these activities imagines that they will make the transition from non-writer to writer in an effortless and natural way. No-one stops to ask what it means in our world to be without talent and yet driven by the need. The criterion for a work of art, after all, he said, is that it should be well made, well finished, and completely severed from its confused and all-too-human origins. And that is only natural, he said. We do not hire a carpenter to make a chair who cannot get the legs straight because of his unhappy childhood, or a mason to build a wall who cannot lay bricks properly because his daughter is a drug addict. By the same token, he said, we would be extremely foolish to pay a writer or a painter for his or her work if they cannot write or paint. At the same time, he said, and asked me if I would have another and got up and

Gabriel Josipovici   87

went to the bar and came back with the drinks and sat down again, at the same time, he said, I cannot tell you the sense of relief, of exhilaration even, which overwhelmed me when I first read the lines: 'On Margate sands I can connect/nothing with nothing./ The broken finger-nails of dirty hands...' Here, I thought, he said, is someone writing about me. Here is someone who understands me. And that after all is what we ask from writing, that it should speak to us and about us. The broken fingernails of dirty hands, he said, and drank half his beer down and set the glass on the table and looked out of the window at the rain and the river. Of course, he said, I am well aware of the dangers of embracing this as a full-blooded aesthetic, for once the point has been made, what else is there to say? And then a part of me, he said, hankers after a great and complex work, a vast layered labyrinthine construction, into which I can pour all my life and energy. It will have to be different from the great works of the past, he said, but it will have to have the ability to stand up by itself, to allow itself to be picked up and turned round in the hand, as it were, and always to let off a genuine sparkle. I believe in that as well, he said, just as much as I believe in the broken fingernails of dirty hands. So it is like a stone round my neck or a mountain on my back. There are times, he said, like today, when the thought of what I want to do crushes and stupefies me. And then I need to talk to someone, to walk with someone. I cannot advance, he said, and I cannot retreat, and I cannot step to one side and pretend it is none of my business. The truth of the matter is, he said, that I simply do not know how to handle it. In earlier years, he said, when I was young and brash and perhaps innocent, I would have had a go and then, if it proved really intractable, have left it for something else. Perhaps, he said, it is not so much a question of innocence as the sense that one has time, that one is only beginning, that one is allowed to make mistakes, that even if one gets it wrong that is only natural and that gradually as one matures things will start to come right. But one does not mature, he said, one only grows tired more easily and the blows one has taken weaken one's resolve and dampen the hope without which nothing can be achieved. One becomes more inflexible. One's ability to think laterally starts to desert one. Even when one knows one is barking up the wrong tree it seems to require too much of an effort to switch tree. And after all, how would one know which the right tree was? Every day, he said, I am convinced I will find a way of dealing with it, and by the end of the day I am exactly where I was when I started. I have tried getting on with other projects, he said, and letting it ripen in its own good time, but far from ripening it remained stubbornly what it had always been. I have tried thinking about nothing else for seven days and nights. Nothing. I cannot move forward with it and I cannot do anything else except try to move forward. I used to think, he said, that if there was a problem there was a solution. I know that what this really means is that you can always find ways of convincing yourself that you have solved a problem when you've done no such thing. When you are young, he said, you can find ways of lulling your critical spirit to sleep in order to make your life easier. But now I no longer wish to fool myself in this way, or perhaps I have lost the knack of how to fool myself in this way. A time comes, he said, when you realise that it will *not* be better next time, that either there will be no next time or it will be exactly as bad as the previous time. So that even if part of me still believes that the only way forward is to blind myself to these facts and just work, I still cannot do so. Is that what maturity means? he asked. Not wisdom, not understanding, but the growing inability to let things be, a growing hardness with yourself, which might be admirable if there was not always a little voice whispering that it was a sign of the coming end. There comes to every writer, he said, at some time in his life, the idea that he will write one work which will finally justify him, one work into which he can pour himself for as long as it takes, a decade perhaps, or two, or the rest of his life, as with Proust and Dante. But perhaps, he said, that is one of these pernicious legacies Proust and Joyce and Musil have left us. We are not all Joyces or

Gabriel Josipovici 89

Prousts or Musils, nor should we want to be. One of each is quite enough. But the feeling persists, he said, that somehow, somewhere, it is waiting for you, this massive work, and that you will not be able to live with yourself if you do not go out to meet it. It is perhaps a foolish belief, he said, it is quite probably a pernicious belief, but it is there and you have to accept it. I have always felt, he said, that the artist's task was to accept whatever that voice inside him told him and try to be true to it. The trouble is, he said as we left the Star and Garter, that I am at the stage when I begin to wonder if I will ever be true to it, and what the *it* is that I have to be true to. I have lived with it for so long, he said – we were strolling through Holland Park that day – that it has become a part of me, but an unhealthy, stunted part. He had wanted to see the new Japanese garden and was not slow to vent his disappointment. A lot of writing in Japanese on brass tablets and then, in English: *Welcome to the Kyoto Garden. This is a place of beauty and tranquility.* Why more tranquil and beautiful than it was before? he said. And when you are told something is tranquil and beautiful don't you want to start screaming? We sat and listened to the water trickling into the little pond. Moor Park, he said. Animal Languages is another title I thought of. Both convey the idea of limits, edges, between moorland and park-land, between that which can be spoken about and that which lies beyond speech. Moor Park, he said. Like a chimp talking. At first they thought that with enough effort you could teach chimps to talk, he said. They did not realise that the upright posture of man is what makes speech possible. The sound pipes are uninterrupted as they descend from the neck. This is not the case with chimps, even though genetically we differ from them by less than one per cent. But then they realised that speech and language are not necessarily connected so they started teaching them to play with computers and to use the sign language of the deaf. That led to immediate and spectacular success, for the chimps were signing like mad and the observers were having trouble getting all the information down. Unfortunately as time went by it became

obvious that the chimps weren't going to advance much beyond the linguistic horizon of a three year old human child.
At the same time critics were accusing the chimp-language
enthusiasts of fabricating even the evidence they did have
and bitter rows broke out in the scientific community, essentially between those who followed Chomsky and believed
language was innate and basically a question of structure and
those who believed language was acquired piecemeal by
direct reference to the outside world. No-one seemed to see
that we all only develop the kind of language we need, and
that goes for animals as well. I had thought of using as an
epigraph Wittgenstein's devastating remark, 'If a lion could
speak we would not understand what he was saying', but that
now seems to me so obvious that only a scientist obsessed
with teaching apes to use language would overlook it. Come,
he said, I cannot bear this Japonaiserie, and we began to walk
through the park, listening to the unpleasant screech of the
peacocks and peering over the fences at the squirrels. On one
fence-post a squirrel was sitting with its tail over its head,
carefully eating a piece of biscuit held delicately between two
paws, for all the world like a child eating sweet corn. I do not
know what to do, he said. I cannot concentrate on anything
else and yet I cannot concentrate on this. I have written more
than eight hundred pages in the last four years, he said, all
rubbish. I have devised over two hundred different plans, all
rubbish. Am I going to go on like this for the rest of my life?
What a curious destiny it is we suddenly find ourselves con-
fronted with, he said, not at all what we had expected in our
youth. Why, he said as we began to walk again, are we so
obsessed with this idea of a long slow work which we will
perhaps never finish in our lifetime but to which we are committed body and soul? Every morning we get up and sit down
at our desk and we work all day and sometimes well into the
night. We read over what we have written. We tear it up. We
start again. We read that over. We tear it up. We start again.
And slowly it begins to find its rightful form. Slowly it starts
to grow. When we die it is there, unfinished but nevertheless

substantial, a substantial work. Everybody marvels. The patience, they say. The commitment. The dedication. And nobody knew. All done quietly, in the dark. And now we see that it was all worth it, the work, the silence, the dedication. Pah! he said, how can grown men and women be taken in by this drivel? By this sentimentality? The only explanation I can come up with, he said, is our need for redemption, a need, in a secular age, to feel that even if life has not managed to make much sense to us that is only because we haven't had the dedication, the patience, the spark of genius. But at least *someone else has* and so life is meaningful after all. In the old romantic days, he said as we passed the belvedere for the second time, you set the spirit against the flesh, art against the material world. But can we still seriously think in those terms? No, he said, of course we can't. And yet we can't treat art simply as a commodity either, we *know* that there is more to life than the needs of the flesh and the making of money but we do not know how to find that more and imagine that art has the answer. Hopeless confusion, he said, hopeless confusion. We went into the café and joined the queue. There is a country somewhere, he said, somewhere between cynicism and idealism, waiting to be explored. It is a vast country. An unimaginably varied and beautiful country. You wake up and think you now know how to enter it. Then you sit down at your desk and the road vanishes. You are back with the old clichés. The old failures. Human dignity, he said. That is what we need to uphold. But what is more ridiculous than the man who insists on his dignity? No, he said, we can only uphold it by being what we are, by doing what it is in us to do. The body must be tired out, he said, if the mind is doing to yield what it has in it to yield. You have to walk till you drop sometimes, he said, and then pick yourself up and go home and sit in your chair and start to work again. Of course, he said, most of the time this has no effect, you sit in your chair and you are so tired you find yourself falling asleep. But at least you are giving yourself a chance, whereas if you stay indoors all day you have no chance at all. This is the most delightful park in London, he said as we sat on the terrace with our coffees. It is not the most beautiful, Hyde Park is that. It is not the most varied, Hampstead Heath is that. But it is the most delightful, the most charming. Malamud said that not till his very last books did he start to write about his own world, he said, until then he had written, without realising it, about the world of his father. But that is only natural. We all think of life as the life our parents lived, because we are all imitators by nature and we cannot see what others have not seen before us, even when it is staring us in the face. Then, he said, at the end of our lives, if we are lucky, we suddenly say: So this is my life, my very own life, this is what it was, this is what it is. But even that insight has to come by way of our parents, he said, by way of the past. I think of the great parks in cities as belonging to the world of my parents, he said, or even of my grandparents, the world of Europe before the First World War. We feel, he said, that if we can live the lives of our grandparents then in some strange way we are really living. What is happening in our own time does not seem real, not really real. We sense we should leave it to journalists to describe it and report on it, it is not what we feel to be essential, enduring. Writers who are in too much of a hurry to tell us what the present-day world is like seem to us thin and often hollow. There is a mystery there, he said, and I will not try to fathom it. But it seems to be the case that writing that is too concerned with the immediate present quickly passes into oblivion, whereas writing which is not so concerned has a better chance of surviving. On the other hand writing which is unaware of the present and its imperatives is still-born. It is not, he said, that writing deals with a platonic essence, an unchanging human nature, but that the writer, in a curious way, can only invest emotion and imagination in trying to grasp a world in the process of vanishing even as he writes. It is as if the intention of Proust and Kafka, like that of Cervantes and Sterne, he said, was to imagine themselves into a world which had been there when they arrived and so was in a sense guaranteed, and at the same time – and this is surely an index of their greatness – to reveal (and to themselves first of all) that they were forever debarred from that world. It is as if they can only feel themselves alive, he said, to the extent that they feel themselves excluded. And yet those who would blithely accept that exclusion and turn away to colonise the new territory which is theirs and theirs alone seem to leave us with nothing but dust and ashes, or, as Beckett so memorably put it when talking about Balzac, nothing but mechanised cabbages. The Impressionists, he said, were the first to understand the true nature of the open spaces in and around cities. They did not want to paint narratives, especially the narratives of the historians and the mythologists, but rather what those narratives necessarily leave out, cannot accommodate, which, they sensed, today is to be found not in the wilderness and not in city centres but at the edges of cities, where working people spend their leisure. There is something frenetic, he said, about the paintings of inner city life, especially those German paintings of Berlin and Dresden in the inter-war years. That is satire, he said, that is caricature, that is apocalypse. But in the best work of the Impressionists, he said, you can feel what it means to be a human being in a big city, you can feel what it means to be *embodied* even under the pressure of modern urban life. But of course reproduction has ruined the Impressionists for us, he said, just as reproduction has ruined Mozart and Beethoven. We cannot look at the work of the Impressionists, he said, after all the postcards and the posters, all the chocolate boxes and the calendars. I am not a person who feels at home in the heart of the big cities, he said, in the hustling bustling metropolitan centres. I like the parks and the cemeteries, the sense of an oasis of peace in the middle of the frenzy, the Luxembourg Gardens, Père Lachaise, Brompton Cemetery, Primrose Hill, the walks round the lakes in Hamburg and Berlin. But that is the world of my grandparents, he said, I feel their ghosts haunting the alleys and the little garden cafés. For a Jew, he said, such places are always tinged with melancholy, they always represent the spaces between, where one is neither rooted nor rootless, part of a city and yet not a part of it, a breathing space where the mind can wander as the body wanders. For my mother's parents, he said, England was a dream which affected their lives as only dreams can. Can you believe it, he said, they only visited England once in their lives and that was to buy their wedding furniture at Maples, this Jewish doctor from Odessa and his wife, the daughter of a Jewish lawyer from Ferrara. Doesn't that tell you something about history? That they should come all the way from Egypt, where no doubt they could have acquired perfectly adequate furniture if they had wanted it, to choose their furniture in Maples in London? And an English governess, he said. My mother's first language was English, though that of her mother was French and of her father Russian, and the reason for that was her gaunt and upright English governess. Who was of course, as was the way in those days, much closer to her than her own mother, and who taught her Anglican prayers and quoted Shakespeare, the Bible and Dr Johnson at her. A fool would have swallowed it, Dr Johnson said, said the nanny when the little girls spat out a piece of food that was too hot. She quoted Dr Johnson so often and in connection with such everyday matters, my mother told me, he said, that we were convinced he was a doctor friend of hers. Think of it, he said, a little Jewish girl whose grandfather was a tea-merchant in Odessa, brought up on Anglican prayers and snippets from Shakespeare and Dr Johnson in a spa town ten miles south of Cairo. That tells you something about the world of 1910, he said. And now in 1988, he said, I am past fifty and have been in this country for over thirty years and yet I still find England a puzzle, still walk in the parks and still struggle to make sense of what it is I want out of life and what it is I need in order to function properly. Shakespeare seems much closer to me than George Eliot, he said, but Proust is closest of all, perhaps because Proust seems to embody that world of 1910, not nostalgically but in all its complexity and contradiction, like a much wiser and more articulate version of my grandparents whom I never knew. When one begins to write, he said as we left the little open-air café in Holland Park, one wants to make something that will stand on its own two feet and if only one can do that one is satisfied. But after a while, he said, one wants to do something bigger, something that will engage and commit one fully. For a long time, as you know, he said, I resisted this. I thought of it as a trap and a temptation. I saw what happened to quite promising writers who decided in middle age to write the masterpiece that would bring them fame and wealth and who succeeded only in producing a load of indigestible rubbish. Writers claim that they are concerned with the environment, he said. You have only to read the letters to the editor and the full-page adverts about saving the rain-forest and protecting the ozone layer and all the rest of it, and you will see that writers are up there in the front line, the famous ones, the ones with clout, defending the environment. And yet, he said, it is writers who do more than anyone else to contribute to the deforestation of this planet, and then do not do it incidentally, by some sort of chance, he said, they actually put all their fearsome energy into it, writing bigger and bigger books and trying to get more and more copies printed, not noticing that their ambition and their ideals simply cannot be reconciled. Until we finally hit on ways of making paper that does not involve cutting down trees, he said, that contradiction will remain. That is one reason, he said, why a Mallarmé, a Borges, appeals to me so much. After them, he said, there is absolutely no excuse for writing a long book, scarcely any excuse for writing books at all, no excuse for going on and on about deforestation and ozone layers and at the same time contributing to it all by the printing of more and more and longer and longer books. One sentence a year, he said, we should ration writers to one sentence a year, and then at least we might get some interesting sentences, and the reading public would read these interesting sentences with the attention they would no doubt require. As for publishers, he said, they are already so busy revamping books that have gone out of copyright and reprinting in ever shoddier editions books every civilised person will have read in the delightful old Everyman and Worlds Classics editions, the less said about them the better. Or else, he said, and that is the solution I have often thought might work best, we should make writers grow the very trees that will be used to make the paper for the books they write, that would teach them the value of words. Of course, he said, I am to blame as much as anyone, but then I have never professed any commitment to green issues, and my books can hardly be accused of diminishing by very much the world's fragile resources. And yet, he said, the common ambition has taken hold of me too, perhaps that is why the stone lies so heavily on my back, the world is taking its revenge as in the old days Venus took her revenge on those who had slighted the notion of love. Moor Park, he said, the country house of Sir William Temple, Swift's employer. Not to be confused with another and older country house of the same name, the residence of the Countess of Bedford, friend of Donne and Herbert, Moor Park in Hertfordshire. That was the inspiration behind William Temple's own house and garden, to which the former diplomat, now retired, moved from Sheen in the 1680's, Moor Park in Surrey near Guildford. Now a part of the university of Surrey. At one time a lunatic asylum. Also a college of theology and, during the war, the home of one of the code-breaking units to which Alan Turing was briefly attached. Even, for a few years, in the sixties, an experimental centre for the study of primates, linked to the famous Institute for Primate studies at Norman, Oklahoma, home of Washoe, Lucy and many other language-learning chimps. In the time of Sir William Temple, he said as we left Holland Park by the High Street Kensington gate, it was famous for its gardens, and Sir William himself wrote a distinguished essay on gardens, part of the growing English interest in Italian and Dutch garden design and a powerful voice in the debate on how far to retain the tradition of informal formality or formal informality for which the Italians and the Dutch were renowned, and how far to go over to the rigorous geometrical formality of the French garden. Gardens, he said, as we turned into

Kensington Church Road, the history of gardens. From Babylon to the present. From China to Italy, Iceland to Peru. If we could understand what gardens have meant to people, what humanity has tried to express in the form of the garden, he said, we would understand a great deal more about ourselves. The trouble with most studies of primate behaviour, he said, is that they start from the assumption that it is the behaviour of the apes that has to be explained. But it is our own behaviour that is really much more puzzling. And that is what apes can help us to see, he said. And not only apes. The great crested grebe, in Huxley's famous study, the bee as examined by von Frisch, the ant via the extraordinary work of Eugène Marais. And why stop at animals? he said. We should not only write a history of the cultivation and use of the potato *by* man, but a parallel history of man *and* the potato. The garden as metaphor, he said. The garden as refuge. The garden as the expression of man's need to dominate. The garden as Paradise. The closed garden. The open garden. The garden as a place of healing. The garden as a means of exploration. The orchard. The meadow. The rock garden. Already walking round the Serpentine the previous year he had expatiated on gardens. He had suggested that we should treat gardens as gestures and create an index of such gestures, like Stith-Thompson's index of folk-motifs. Though gardens figure quite extensively in the Bible, he said, we Jews, for obvious reasons, have never felt much at home in gardens or had much interest in or knowledge of them. The garden is a sign of continuity, he said, a sign of settlement. That is why Jeremiah knows no better way to signal his trust in a God who will keep the great powers from invading Israel than by planting fruit trees in an orchard. But the days of Jeremiah are long past, he said. Even my family, which was a family of means once, though not of wealth, left gardening strictly to the gardener. Someone like me, he said, who has never felt at home in any country or in any city in which he has lived, cannot conceive of growing things in my own garden. Even someone like me, who loves nature and never feels happier than when walking through fields and under trees, cannot conceive of planting and tending a garden. For, as Jeremiah saw, that seems to suggest that you have time, that you have a future, and that is the one thing I do not feel I have and have never felt I had. When I have had gardens I have enjoyed them, he said, but I have not known how to look after them and they have all, sooner or later, gone to seed. *Carcere d'invenzione*, he said as we went into the café on the river for a cup of tea, the prison-house of invention. Piranesi's title and etchings, he said, will form the basis of my book, the utmost stretches of the mind, the mind stretched to breaking-point, and then the book turns inside-out like a glove, revealing itself only as the prison-house of the imagination. The subject fills me with joy, he said, more joy than I have felt for any project since I wrote my first novel. Prisons alone, he said, or the thought of them, can only fill one with despair. Invention alone, ditto, because the absence of limits is always melancholy. But bring the two together, as Piranesi has in his title, and everything is transformed. The imagination not as freedom but constraint. And in the end the sense of freedom achieved through the act of imprisoning invention. An idea without a form, he said, is worse than useless, and so is a form without content. Only when the two come together can a work of value ensue. And in that title, *Carcere d'invenzione*, he said, the two do indeed come together, giving me hope that here at last is the germ of what I have wanted to settle down to for so long. I have been flailing about for such a long time, he said, knowing what I wanted but not knowing how to set about achieving it. But now, he said, everything is beginning to fall into place. It's a bit like an hourglass, he said, and suggested we have another cup of tea, the sand seeps slowly from one part of the glass to the other, and as the one fills up so the other empties. It is the same with the making of a work of art, he said. The life passes from the maker who has so far not been able to put it to any use, into the work, which grows and becomes strong and goes on growing, if all goes well, until all the life that was in the creator has gone into the work. But the paradox of creative work, he said, is that when the work is finished it is the life of the maker which is renewed. As though only by giving birth in this way could you replenish yourself. No-one has explained this satisfactorily, he said, and no-one is likely to, nor should we really want anyone to do so. But every maker knows what I am talking about, and can vouch for the truth of what I have just said. And it is not when the work is finished that the maker finds himself filled with a new lease of life, but as he works at it, as the sand drains from him into the work, that he is himself replenished. Without the chance to give in this way we would not be able to receive. What is yours to bestow is not yours to reserve, Shakespeare has one of his characters say. He is talking about love and sexual favours, but what he says holds true of the making of art as well. For the dialectic of living and reserving, of holding and losing, living and gaining, is one which applies to every aspect of life. *Carcere d'invenzione*, he said, examining the underside of his plastic cup, the spark I have been looking for for a long time. It is all a matter of confidence, he said as we set out once more, just as it is in sport, football, say, or tennis. If you are confident, he said, you relax, you go for your shots, you sense instinctively when to move and when to hold back. When you lack confidence you become tentative, you begin to look at yourself from the outside, become conscious of the spectators, start to worry about whether you can make the shots, pass the ball, and so you lose your instinctive sense of what is happening outside and beyond you, of the man on the other side of the net, of the rest of the players on the pitch. But it is precisely your sense of this, your intuitive sense of this, that has made you the player you are. It is the same with writing, he said. Once you begin to worry about what you are going to achieve or what people are going to say, you lose your instinctive rhythm, you lose your ability to pick up the vibrations from what has gone before and so your ability to surge forward. There is no mystery in it, he said. It was what Keats admired in Shakespeare and Nietzsche in Goethe. When you are confident, he said, everything falls into your lap. Not complacent, he said, but confident. The difference between the two states is absolute. To be complacent is to *expect* things to fall into your lap. It is to imagine that everything you do is perfect. To be confident is to know by instinct when to press and when to hold back, when to work and when to rest. It is to be able to dare and not to be constantly seeking to surprise. Of course, he said, even the most confident sometimes feel a tinge of doubt, but that is as it should be, confidence does not mean foolhardiness. It is not by watching a game of tennis that we improve, he said, it is by playing. And the same is true of writing. However many ideas you have before you start, once you begin to write everything changes and everything depends on your instinct and your confidence and the depth of your understanding, not on your learning or your intelligence or the number of notes you have taken. Talking is natural, he said, as we paused to let a group of riders go by, but writing? Perhaps, though, he said, as we began to walk again, it all depends on one's perspective. Making sounds is natural, one could say, but talking is artificial. The human animal, he said, defers pleasure in order to acquire a greater good. The child denies itself the pleasure of merely laughing or crying at a certain point in its development, and accepts instead to call: ma-ma, da-da. The consonant requires an effort, it requires an acceptance of the curtailment of the lovely sensation of the open throat. But the introduction of the consonant is the beginning of language. Mama, the child calls, and the mother comes. Give ball, the child says, and the mother complies. He who would speech find about must and about must go. It is the same with writing. I deny myself the pleasure and relief of simply howling in order to gain the greater and more lasting pleasure of making something that will still be there when I return to it, something *I* will have made, which did not exist before I made it and would not ever have existed had I not made it. Not that any writer ever re-reads what he has written once it is done, he said, and that is a curious and interesting fact in itself. It is as though after all the effort, after the blood sweat and tears of making, once the thing is made it can be forgotten and something else will take its place as a focus for my passion. But made for what purpose? Not in order to fortify my house, like the beaver, or to acquire food, like the chimp. Perhaps, he said, it has to do with control and yet also with letting go, with finding a rhythm that is more satisfactory than the ordinary rhythm of life. But in the end who can explain it? I am glad you have no truck with aesthetics, he said. Aesthetics is a waste of time. Logic on the other hand, he said, like mathematics, is closely related to art. To be a logician or a mathematician, he said, is to be a maker, not a parasite. In 1711, he said, the ponds in the London Parks froze over and Londoners spent their days skating. Swift wrote to Stella about it, in between giving her his tedious and boring news about the political machinations of the time and what grandee he had dined with and what minister he had supped with. Swift, he said, was the most interesting as well as the most boring man who ever lived. The most vain and the most humble. The most whimsical and the most heavy-handed. The most closed and the most open. He belongs so thoroughly to English and Anglo-Irish society of the early eighteenth century that only a historian of the period could find much of his writing of any interest, but he also belongs to the larger European world of the late Renaissance and in many ways he is closer to it than almost any other figure before Wordsworth, Coleridge and Keats. In the same letter in which he informs Stella that he has seen the skaters on the pond of St James', he said, he tells her he has bought a copy of Aristophanes, and this copy, a folio volume, a copy of the edition printed in Geneva in 1607, was in his library when he died. 'I laid out one pound five shillings for a Strabo and an Aristophanes,' he tells her, 'and I have now got books enough to make me another shelf, and I will have more.' In these letters back to Stella from London, he said, where he was spending his time hobnobbing with Prime Ministers and Secretaries of State, he had to tread a careful line between a silence which would have offended and too frequent a mention of Vanessa, which would have roused Stella's suspicions. A man of over forty, he said, with a dozen brilliant books behind him, including one of the greatest books in the English language, *A Tale of a Tub*, and yet he acts towards her like an adolescent on the town for the first time and writing to his girl back home. And he never changes, he said as we turned into Kensington Gardens by the Serpentine Galleries and went down to the river path. His life is living proof that we do not mature, he said, that time does not bring wisdom, that we understand ourselves no better at sixty than at twenty. 'My poetical fountain is drained,' he writes to Pope in 1732, when he was sixty-five, 'and I profess I grow gradually so dry, that a rhyme with me is almost as hard to find as a guinea, and even prose speculations tire me almost as much.' Yet, like the inveterate writer that he is, he adds that he does have a couple of things he's been working on for years, that these are terrible and he has no intention of sending them to Pope but perhaps one day he will get them finished. He is referring to his wonderful *Polite Conversations* and *Directions to Servants*, masterpieces of observation and irony. Swift's life and his books, he said as we reached the river again, are a rebuke to the whole tradition of the novel, of the *bildungsroman* in particular. His books are as angry as the plays of John Osborne, he said, but anger is only a small part of it. They are dry, he said, and that is what I love about them. All art can be divided into two, he said, the wet and the dry. Aristophanes is dry, Euripides is wet. Homer is dry, Virgil is wet. Dante and Chaucer are dry but Petrarch and Wyatt are wet. Donne is dry but Milton is wet. Jane Austen is dry but George Eliot and Goethe are both wet. Sterne is a complicated case, he said, wetness miming dryness miming wetness, or perhaps dryness miming wetness miming dryness. Shakespeare, as usual, defies the categories, he said, the murder of Macduff's children is wet and so is much of *Cymbeline* and *The Tempest* and *Othello* and *Lear*. But he gets away with it, he said, because you can never tell if he is wet himself or only dramatising wetness. Ivy Compton-Burnett is dry, he said, and E. M. Forster is wet. Coleridge, strangely, is dry, and Wordsworth wet. By and large though the nineteenth century is wholly wet. In England at any rate. You can be sure that all the winners of prizes will be wet, for the judges are invariably wet. Nature is dry and man is wet he said as we rounded the lake and stopped to look at the ducks. In Dogen's great *Sutra on Mountains and Rivers*, he said, the point is made that water is the embodiment of the principle of enlightenment, for form is emptiness and emptiness is form, form is empty and transcended when it becomes actual and momentarily pools time and space. That is why you invariably find in Japanese gardens a thin unobtrusive thread of water that momentarily forms into a pool and then continues on its journey. That is what our art should be like, he said, the pool and the stream with it, not the pool alone or the stream alone but the pool and the stream together. When an idea hits me, he said, an idea for a story or a novel or a play, then it nearly always takes this form, the stream and the pool, the joy or sorrow of the individual life and the continuity in which that life is embedded, the millennia that have passed before and the millennia that will pass after it. Perhaps such thoughts of the fragility of things, of the temporary nature of even the most solid-seeming things, arise more easily in someone like myself, he said, someone who has no homeland and no possibility of ever acquiring one and no nostalgia for anything lost. Such feelings are bound to occur with less force and more rarely to those who have somewhere they feel they have come from and to which they can return, and perhaps to them what I am concerned with seems meaningless or esoteric. One can only do what one is driven to do, he said, the great betrayal is to try and do what you think you should do or what you think people expect of you or what you think will bring you success. Such actions not only destroy your own soul, which is after all strictly your own business and does not concern anyone else, but they are also responsible for the great mass of what is written and painted and composed, that turgid torrent that pours down over us and filthies us and paralyses us. We can try and take evasive action, he said, you and I, we know how to defend ourselves against it, but for the young and the confused and the easily influence-able it is not so easy. Today what models are they asked to follow? he said. I will not mention names but you know what I mean. Forster and Greene were bad enough, he said, but if their art is not up to much at least it has integrity. Today in the majority of cases our writers have substituted self-right-eousness for integrity, they flow with the filthy tide and talk of subversion and risk. It is laughable, he said, to hear them talk on television and in newspaper interviews about how they are vilified and silenced and how the authorities deny them a voice. I would not like to be young today, he said. I am glad I was born when I was and came to England when I did. It was bad enough being young then but today it is much worse, he said. The young do not know what to do with their lives and they are bombarded on every side by appeals to their cupidity and greed or by a naive morality based on anger and resentment. The idea that self-sacrifice and renunciation might in itself bring happiness does not enter into their minds, he said, time has been devalued, integrity has been devalued, men and women behave like animals and are re-warded for it. An animal acts according to its instincts, he said, but to act *like* an animal and yet no longer have animal in-stincts is to create a living hell. It is not the fault of the young, he said, it is the fault of my generation for peddling such panaceas. People have become incapable of sustained effort, incapable of quiet growth, incapable of patience, incapable of endurance. When one looks at what the so-called civilised world has come to, he said, one despairs of making anything because it is certain to be ignored. But one must make that effort, one must go on doing what one knows is good, he said, one must turn one's eyes away from the world and focus only on what it is that has to be done. *Carcere d'invenzione*, he said to me as we sat in the open-air café in Kew Gardens, the prison-house of invention. That is the only theme left for us today – or for me at any rate, who am I to speak for the world? And perhaps, he said, that is what all my work has been about till now, but the time has come to face it head on. Each work one starts must be thought of as the final one, the last and the best, he said, the last thing one will ever do and that towards which all one has ever done has always been tending. Swift, he said. The young Swift who tended Sir William Temple as his secretary at Moor Park and there met Stella, only eight years old, the age of Beatrice when Dante first saw her. Was she the illegitimate child of Sir William, as some have suggested? Was Swift? If both these postulates are true that would make them half brother and sister and might explain much in their relationship. Unfortunately it seems probable that neither is true and that the suggestion is the product of a silly and sentimental age. As if their relationship was not interesting enough as it stands. She was eight and he in his early twenties. Though not formally her tutor he took a great interest in her education and, he later told her, she made an apt pupil. When she lay dying he was away in England. He hurried to get back to her but the boat was held up by storms off Holyhead and he had to hang about in a country inn, biting his nails and going for long walks in the driving rain. When he finally arrived in Dublin she was dead. He would not attend her funeral though he was closer to her, he writes in a letter, than to any other human being and her death was, he said, the most important event in his life. He sat in the Deanery night after night, jotting down his memories of her. Not in his own study, which gave onto the churchyard, but in a little room at the back. Why did he not attend her funeral? Was it more painful for him than it usually is for the bereaved? Did he not wish to draw attention to their relationship? But everyone knew they were close friends, if not more. Did not his absence draw more attention to it than his presence would have done? Surely we can take him at his word and accept that he simply could not. But what does simply could not mean here? Can anyone? But they do. Yet he refused. And his refusal has passed down into history. The old Swift, he said, so deaf that Pope said he had started *The*

Dunciad to while away the time because he could not converse with his guest, and prone to fall suddenly to the ground because of a disease of the ear which played havoc with his balance. The cause, he always claimed, had been the immoderate eating of fruit one summer in his youth, an explanation which sounds more Christian than medically sound. He writes to a friend that having ridden eight miles out of Dublin in search of exercise he suddenly felt funny and had to be taken into a house and made to lie down until he could be fetched back home. One feels, he said, as one reads these painful letters of the seventeen thirties that Swift, who in his younger days had always relished a fight with the establishment if anything he believed in was being dealt with in a manner he considered unfair, was now wrestling with an enemy mere powerful and malignant even than Sir Robert Walpole, an enemy who would always have the last word. But however often Swift was thrown to the ground, he would always get up and continue the struggle. Swift the learned wit, he said, fascinated by unknown languages, by animal languages, by the mirage of a universal language which would in one fell swoop undo the damage of Babel and the Fall itself. I have always thought, he said, that *Gulliver's Travels*, quite as much as *The Dunciad*, is meant to be an ironic inversion of *Paradise Lost*, its message that we will lose everything, even what we have, if we imagine we can ever regain paradise on earth. So, he said, Swift at Moor Park, listening to the smug if not pompous Sir William Temple pontificate about everything under the sun, from the right way to bring peace to Europe to the best way of growing pears, Swift listening to the noble lord talking about all this and agreeing with him and admiring his wealth, his culture, his easy access to the centres of power and to the riches of tradition, and yet feeling obscurely that something was wrong, that matters were not as simple as Sir William was making out, that the ice on which he skated so elegantly was thinner than he imagined and might at any moment break and precipitate not only the noble lord but all he stood for into the cold dark waters. Swift listening to all this and keeping his peace, he said, but listening too to Stella learning her lessons and then instructing her what books to read, what writers to imitate, how to form her characters and her character. Swift in middle age in exile in Ireland, far from his friends, far from the court at which he had once been an honoured guest, exchanging macaronic verses with the schoolmaster Delaney, complaining to his friends in England about the bitterness of his exile yet unwilling to change a way of life which after all had come to suit him. Swift in his last years, his memory gone, unable to find the words he wanted and, after an angry search, relapsing into silence or into the unhappy comment, 'I am a fool', or rocking in his chair and repeating to himself, over and over, 'I am what I am, I am what I am'. Those great estates like Moor Park, he said. Some of them still exist today, they are photographed for books on eighteenth-century history and society, on the history of the garden, on gardens and literature. But how many of these books stop to ask about the gardeners who kept the hedges trim, who watered the plants and cleaned out the grottoes, or the many servants who made it possible for the big house to function? The rule for such people was invisibility, he said. They had to do their allotted task as perfectly as possible. To be noticed was to have made a mistake. But Swift noticed them. His wonderfully ironic *Directions to Servants* tells us more than any other document of the time about the hardships and tribulations of these people, and about their methods of revenge on those who employed them and exercised such casual power over them. 'When you have done a fault,' he advises, 'be always pert and insolent, and behave yourself as if you were the injured person; this will immediately put your master or lady off their mettle.' Or: 'Always lock up the cat in the closet where you keep your china plates, for fear the mice may steal in and break them.' Swift's insights, of course, he said, were the result not only of his keen sense of observation but of his own ambiguous position. At the end of his life, when he wrote the *Directions*, he was the employer of many servants. But in his youth at Moor Park matters had been a little different, and he, who forgot nothing, would not have forgotten this. As far as he was concerned he was Sir William's secretary and confidant, but as far as Sir William and his sister, Lady Giffard, were concerned, he was merely another employee. Stella's role in the household was more ambiguous, he said. No-one quite knows on which side of the salt she sat, though most probably she and her chaperone, Dingley – wonderful Dickensian name – came into the category of 'poor relations', a large category, precisely designed to leave the status of such persons ambiguous, neither masters nor servants, not required to help in the servicing of the house and grounds, but as dependent as the servants on the good will of master and mistress. In some ways, he said, it was a more invidious position than that of the butler and the gardeners, because they at least had precise tasks to carry out and if they did them well they were reasonably secure. But the poor relation had nothing to do and no way of knowing whether she was allaying or fuelling the master's displeasure by her presence. Totally dependent on the whim of the master, she could not even take pleasure in the sense of a task well done, as could the gardener and the groom. But was the position of someone like Swift any better? His duties were by no means clear and his own view of them did not always coincide with that of Sir William. What Swift has left us from his Moor Park days, he said that day in the open air café in Kew Gardens, seems on the surface to be nothing but eulogies of his patron, poems of praise, dedications, introductions to his master's letters which he edited after the latter's death and so on and so forth. But one wonders if he did indeed see him as the father he would have liked to have had, as most of his modern biographers have suggested. Is it likely, he said, that a man of Swift's brilliance and ambition would idolise a man like Temple, of whom Burnet wrote that he was 'a vain man, much blown up in his own conceit, which he showed too indecently on all occasions'? Temple, he said, saw himself as a second Sir Philip Sidney, the embodiment of all the renaissance virtues and an effective and tireless champion of

England's interests abroad, whereas we know from others and from what we can read between his own lines that he was a mediocre ambassador and a rather limited and unimaginative specimen of a certain class and a certain period. There was nothing wrong with the humanist ideals of Sir William, he said, the trouble lies with his tone. His essays on gardens and on ancient and modern learning, his lectures on politics, his letters to the great and glorious consist for the most part of platitudes. There is not a thought or even a half-thought there. We agree with his views but cannot help yawning when we read him. If this is truth and virtue, we feel, then give us lies and vice any day. But the heart of the matter, I feel, he said, is that Moor Park and its gardens was for Temple a retreat from the pressures of a world of which he had had enough, an earthly paradise in which he was sole lord and master and where he could conduct his agricultural experiments and compile — with the help of his secretary — the memoirs which would vindicate him to the world. For Swift, on the other hand, it was a most comfortable prison in which he felt his genius shrivel as he did another man's bidding and as the time left to him to make his mark upon the world trickled slowly but remorselessly away. No wonder *A Tale of a Tub*, written almost entirely at Moor Park, reveals fantasies of madness, violence and obscenity. It is, we must feel, what kept him from almost literally blowing up. And what of Stella? Did he feel sorry for her in her position of extreme vulnerability? Or was he moved by her innocence? Or roused by her looks and the difference in their ages? Or, on the contrary, did he feel safe with someone who could not challenge him sexually or emotionally? Biographers have pointed out, he said, and we got up and went to have a look at the greenhouses, for the air was turning a little chill, that he instinctively took on the role of tutor and advisor to all the young women he fell for. But girls do not, alas, remain girls for ever, and yet Swift's relations with her nevertheless endured until her death. If they did marry, he said as we entered the temperate greenhouse, it was the strangest marriage ever contracted, with both partners committed to keeping the union a secret. What did Swift think of her? he said. And what did he think about the way he behaved towards her? We will never know. Eighteenth-century letter-writers tell us very little about their feelings, he said, and even the letters he wrote to her at the height of his influence when, in London, he was dining daily with the most important ministers of state, and which posterity knows as the *Journal to Stella*, tell us more about his daily visits and conversations than about his heart. The PS's he scribbled in that curious baby language which was like the dark side of his polished official prose have proved, on decipherment, to be embarrassingly maudlin, unrelieved by any irony. Or were they? With Swift, he said, it is always impossible to tell. He was what he was. We left the temperate greenhouse and he suggested we go briefly into the palm house. Then there was the question of Vanessa, he said as we entered. He paused as we took off our jackets and made our way down the main aisle. He was obviously drawn to her, he said, she was richer than Stella, an independent woman, and probably more attractive physically. But like Stella she was a young woman with whom it was easy to enter into the role of tutor or uncle. However, he said, he was already so deeply embroiled with Stella that he could not, in the end, make the break he so desired. Guilt or concern, cowardice or gentlemanly behaviour – how shall we describe it? he said as we toiled up the corkscrew iron staircase. No-one will ever know, he said, know even if these terms are at all adequate to the situation. For every situation is unique and, as someone said, the trouble with life is that there are no rehearsals. Stella or Vanessa? he said. Or both? Or neither? In the end, he said, it was too much for Swift. Vanessa was less submissive than Stella, less willing to do things according to his rules. He was horrified when she came alone to visit him where he was staying in Oxford and – he felt – nearly compromised the two of them. He never forgave her for that, the prig, or perhaps he realised that she was simply too dangerous for someone like himself, who needed women but needed to keep them at a playful distance. So, he said, as we started down the corkscrew stairs at the other end, Stella won without even having been aware that a struggle had been taking place. Think, he said as we stopped at the bottom and wiped our brows, what we might have known not just about Swift but about human nature if Swift had been born in the age of Keats and had left us letters like those of Keats. On the other hand, he said, as we moved towards the exit, what I like about Swift is precisely the fact that he was not Keats, that we know so little about what went on inside him and have to infer so much for ourselves. That suits me, he said, it suits my purpose. There is no point in writing about Keats, he said, he has done it so much better himself. And there is no point in writing about Swift as if he was Keats, or someone like him, as nineteenth-century writers were fond of doing. The challenge, he said as we left the palm house, is to find a way of bringing out the non-modern complexity of Swift, the way he escapes our ready-made moulds and so challenges us to revise them. A few minutes in there, he said nodding back to the greenhouse as we put on our jackets, drains all the nonsense out of you. When my work is going badly, he said, I often go in there and sweat it out. It's better than a sauna, and cheaper. When my wife and I separated, he said, I used to come here almost every day and I found it did me the world of good. When I found the teaching growing more and more depressing I would come in here after a day at the university and within a few minutes all the frustration and anger had been sweated out of me. Who would have believed that young people would be so little interested in the things of the spirit? he said as we made our way towards the main exit. And who would have imagined that they could be so tiresomely moralistic? In the sixties, he said, we were told that Puritanism had at last been laid to rest, but to an outsider like me it was obvious that the sixties themselves were simply a further twist on the Puritan spiral, that sexual liberation and flower power were merely the flip side of a rigid Puritanism which is obsessed by the body and which, it seems, will never leave these shores until England is well and truly merged with Europe. And not even then, he said, for England and Europe are now in thrall to America and America will remain a Puritan country for a long time yet. When religion dies morality is waiting to step into its shoes, he said. You can see it happening with Luther and with Milton and with George Eliot. It is the same with Reform Judaism, he said, a movement with which I have much sympathy but which is, in the end, founded on the death of real religious feeling and which, alas, tends to take itself overseriously, as do all religious movements founded on morality and not on ritual. We cannot tolerate old-fashioned religions like Catholicism or Orthodox Judaism, he said, for good and obvious reasons, but instead of turning our backs on the whole religious sphere we invent these versions of liberalism which, like all liberalisms, have the seeds of their own destruction built into them. The trouble with morality, he said as we reached the gate, is that because it is founded on distrust of the self it lacks a sense of humour. You cannot have a sense of humour, he said, when you are constantly checking to see if you are feeling and acting as you should be feeling and acting. Reform Judaism is a little better off, he said, because the history of the Jewish people has taught them to distrust righteousness. But Protestantism equates solemnity with profundity and profundity with truth. Those who instinctively feel that there is something wrong with this have nothing else to fall back on except irony and cynicism. The Anglican church, he said as we boarded a bus for the centre, veers uncomfortably between solemnity and irony, and as a result few take it seriously or are prepared to give it their allegiance. London is indeed becoming a most horrible place, he said as the bus came to a standstill for the sixth time in as many minutes, it is like a cake that is burned on the outside but raw inside. Only its parks and the fact that it is so big that it is bound to have among its inhabitants a few people worth talking to, a few genuine individuals, saves it from being one of the most horrible and depressing places in the world. I had thought of going to live in the country, he said, but where would I go? You cannot just get up and go somewhere for no reason at all, he said, and where would I find a reason? I cannot go back to a familiar spot and I cannot settle near to friends or relatives, for I am not familiar with any of it and I have no friends or relatives. Besides, he said, the country, for at least three hundred miles round London, is nothing but a gigantic suburb of the capital. A gigantic suburb. There are still pockets of resistance he said, but who wants to live in a pocket? It is no better in France and Italy, he said, and in some ways it is much worse, for they are now teeming with holiday cottages and farms and castles owned by the English. We have to face the fact, he said, that the world is rapidly becoming an utterly intolerable place, partly because none of it is hidden any more, for there is nowhere in the world which has not been filmed and televised, it is driving us all mad, those of us who have enough to eat and enough money to pay for a roof over our heads, and of course those who do not have enough to eat and nowhere to live and have been driven out of their homes and their countries. The advantage of the latter over the former, he said, is that they can still hope, whereas for us there is infinite comfort but absolutely no hope. I am not of course suggesting, he said as we got off the bus at South Kensington, that their position is any better than ours or that we should envy them in any way. I hope I have enough imagination to recognise that such a view would be arrogant and insulting nonsense. Nevertheless, he said, hope is a great blessing. The reason Kafka and Benjamin never got to Palestine, he said, is that as long as they could dream about it they could go on hoping. What they feared above all was going to Palestine and finding that things there were no different from anywhere else. That is the difference between a romantic temperament and a classic one, he said, the Romantic defers action out of fear that it will put paid to hope, which is what keeps him going, whereas the Classic acts when he needs to and is driven not by fear or hope but by confidence or trust. Unfortunately such trust is beyond us. And to start again in a new land and find you are not in the earthly paradise you hoped for but only in an impoverished version of the limbo you have just left – anything is better than that, anything. Kafka, he said, was the first person to realise that there really is no hope, no hope at all, that all hope is folly and blindness and deliberate self-betrayal. At the same time, he said, he never lost hope. That is why his work goes on resonating for us when that of most of his contemporaries has fallen into decent obscurity. What we admire so much in Kafka, he said, what, strangely, gives us the courage to go on, is the sense he conveys of absolute purity. The only other writer who conveys that to my knowledge is Dante. We may not understand Kafka, he says, but we only have to read two lines of him to be overwhelmed by this purity. I can do without many things, he said, but Dante and Kafka I cannot do without. Of course I would not die if they were withheld from me, and I would not have died if I had never read them, but without them I would wither, my horizons would shrink, a part of me would die. They remind us of what it is to be truly ourselves, he said, and, unfortunately, except for a few very strong spirits, we most of us need constant reminding of that. I do anyway, he said, and he came back to the subject the next time we met, when we walked along the London canals from Limehouse to Regent's Park, first the Grand Union Canal and then Regent's Canal. It is as though by ourselves, with only the mirror to tell us who we are, he said, even with our loved ones and our colleagues, we soon turn into monsters, soon forget what possibilities for the spirit there are, what we can still do. We need Dante and Rabelais and Kafka and Proust, he said, we need van Eyck and Bonnard and Morandi, we need Dufay and Bach and Beethoven and Stravinsky to remind us of that and to help us in our weakness and our frailty. Most artists do not help us, he said, they hinder us, they lead us astray, they bludgeon us with noise and then leave us with nothing and less than nothing. Only a few artists, he said, and we soon discover which ones for ourselves, have the ability to lead us inward and forward and to make us look with the eye of hope and anticipation at the world and ourselves. Left to our own devices, he said, we grow small and hard and get to hate this small hard thing and end in lethargy and despair. We need the artists who matter to remind us constantly that there are possibilities there, in the world and in ourselves, and that hard work and the deployment of energy do have their rewards. The devil looks to tempt us always with the thought that even these artists are wrong, he said, that even they are misleading and tricking us, but we must close our eyes and ears to the words of the devil and keep doing what we believe in. As the Jewish service for the dead puts it, he said, it is not given to any of us to stand aside from the work to be done and it is not given to any of us to complete it. These old liturgies, he said, contain so much wisdom that we ignore them at our peril, even in these secular days. Those words from the service for the dead, he said, give us all we need to go forward in this life. Even the Anglican liturgy, he said, even that is not to be despised. Its roots go back behind Cranmer to the Fathers of the Church and behind them to a millennium of Jewish traditions. We left the canal at Islington and followed the signs through the gloomy streets. The England I read about before I ever set foot here, he said, was characterised by a number of qualities: high-mindedness, eccentricity, a sense of honour, a sense of humour. For all the debunking that has been going on in the past twenty years, much of it no doubt necessary and valuable, the fact remains that that ethos was distinctive and of a certain quality. True there was a lack of imagination, an appalling condescension towards the lower classes and foreigners, the exploitation of workers and women. But still, in spite of all that, there was a distinctive spirit, going right through society and surfacing clearly at moments of crisis. Without the stand of England against Hitler I would not be here today, he said. It's as simple as that. The English may try to puncture the myth of wartime heroism and comradeship but for some of us it cannot be forgotten. But what has happened since the war, he said, though I'm no sociologist, thank God, seems both clear and sad. The links with America, historical and linguistic, and the loss of Empire with the crisis of identity consequent upon that, have resulted in a swamping of native English values by American ones, but American ones of course lacking the native American virtues of freedom and the mixture of races. The result, he said, has been a disaster. The old values derided and in their place a quite horrible middle class and middle brow greed, bitterness and sentimentality, and the inability to distinguish between the authentic and the fake which makes up the intellectual life of this country today. America of course has not been slow to infiltrate the continent of Europe, he said, we hear of plans to build a Disneyland outside Paris, but the French have opened their arms to the US with a certain condescending irony, amused by its exoticism, confident in the virtues of their own traditions. But the result in England has been quite disastrous, he said as we left the hot and dirty Islington streets and descended once more to the banks of the canal. All these isms, he said, they are nothing but an American import. But the sentimentality, the conviction that to suffer means to be right, that belongs to the common Protestant inheritance of both England and America. What dreariness, he said. What conformity. Civilisation as we know it is dying of sentimentality and inanity and self-pity, he said. And England is in the forefront of it all. I suppose, he said, we must be glad that we grew up, and spent a good part of our lives in a rather more interesting and stimulating environment than that in which these poor kids find themselves today. The only rational thing to do today, he said, is to step down, bow out, go one's own way. I weep inwardly when I let myself dwell on it, he said. I want to raise my voice and howl aloud. But that will change nothing and one might as well do what one can while one can and let the world go to the devil. The thought remains though, he said, that there is something wilful and even perverse in setting oneself so much against the world, but one has to brush that aside and simply go on. Perhaps I should have settled in Israel, he said, while there was still time, but I doubt if I would have felt any more at ease there. The fact of the matter is, he said, that I feel uneasy wherever I am, that I find the values of all countries and societies depressing and degrading. Only with a few individuals, like you, he said, do I feel reasonably comfortable, do I feel that I am not a lonely crank but that what I am doing is worth while and even appreciated. Certainties, he said as we passed Camden Lock and were suddenly engulfed by crowds, certainties are what destroy people and warp their humanity. But how to live with uncertainty? I suppose, he said, that it was the good fortune of our grandparents that they could live with uncertainty, that they had room, so to speak, in which to turn, and common beliefs which acted as a kind of safety net. Perhaps the trouble with that generation, he said, was their smug belief that things would not change, their smug confidence that they need not trouble their heads about the world because all would always be for the best. There is no longer room for that, he said, in England or Israel or anywhere else in the world. At least, he said as we turned into Regents Park, the English have the virtue of leaving you alone, at least a large city like London allows you to wander unobserved and to live in a possibly productive uncertainty. In the end, he said, it is the degree of intensity with which we live that is the test. Do we live like cabbages or do we try to live like human beings? Perhaps, he said, the secret is to try and live like human beings while recognising the absurdity of that aim. Sometimes we only walk for an hour or two, sometimes all day. Nobody has ever to my knowledge been invited to his flat and he pretends that he does not have a telephone. I say pretends because it is clear that on the rare occasions when he does call it is from his house and not from a public call-box, but he has never given anyone his number. Usually, though, he summons one by letter. He does not seem to mind if I don't turn up, never mentions it, even if it has happened on two successive occasions. If I cannot meet him on one occasion I try to make sure that I will be there for the next. I have never known him, until now, to miss an appointment or to be late. If we are to meet in a pub I try to get there early and have a drink on my own before he arrives. Sometimes he is there already, drinking at the bar or at a table in the corner. Sometimes he has a notebook open in front of him and is jotting things down in it with a pencil, so that it has happened that we have been in the same room for several minutes before he notices me. Usually it is I who end up going over to him. Even if he sees me he makes no move, but it is more likely that he does not notice what is going on around him. After a walk with him I find in myself a renewed capacity for work, even when the previous few days or weeks have not been good as far as work is concerned. He has that effect. When I talk to him about the work I am doing he always listens with interest and his comments are usually a good deal more pertinent than those of my colleagues, even though he knows very little about my subject. But I do not want to write here about myself but about him. My family would never have understood why I should have given up being a teacher, he said that day as we left the canal at Regent's Park, especially to indulge in what they would have seen as a frivolous and selfish pursuit, the pursuit of something that is not knowledge and that is not likely to be of any benefit to my fellow men. You have to remember, he said, the perennial Jewish suspicion of the merely creative and the purely personal. This was what made Wittgenstein utter the canard that Jews like himself were not and never could be creative. That was of course before the rise of the Nazis, when even intelligent Jews like Wittgenstein still made remarks about 'the Jews'. In the mid-thirties, though, he said, while he did not come back to these remarks, he gradually came to understand that 'not being creative' could itself perhaps be a form of vision or creation, and so he developed a critique both of his old aims and of Romanticism in general with its absurdly over-optimistic notion of 'the creative'. In my better moments, he said, I like to think that this is a justification for what I too am up to. For was there ever such a foolish activity as this, he said that day in Regent's Park, covering his ears as he did so in order not to hear the cries of the caged birds and the howling of the caged animals, to try and be 'creative' when one is deeply aware of the absurdity of the notion? You have to understand, he said, that alongside the Jewish suspicion of the creative there existed, in my family as in the whole of the bourgeoisie of the time, a kind of mindless admiration for the creative and for the artist. These people, he said, had forgotten their Jewish roots, they had assimilated to such an extent that they had adopted as their own the desires and aspirations of the upper bourgeoisie as it manifested itself at that time throughout the whole of the civilised world. And for many of them, he said, even the events of the thirties, even the war did not really impinge. You must realise, he said, that Egypt, though close to one of the main theatres of the war, did not experience what everyone in Europe experienced, the horror and terror of those times, the sense of the end of something and the sense of the utter helplessness of civilisation in the face of ruthless dictators driven solely by ideology. Thus, he said, those who spent the war in Egypt could never really understand what those like my mother who lived through it in Europe had been through. Even the Suez crisis of 1956, he said, when so many of them were thrown out and had to remake their lives in Rome or Paris or Montreal, was never properly understood by them but only seen as a kind of natural calamity, like an earthquake or a flood, rather than the product of history and the decisions of diplomats and leaders. But for people like myself and my parents, he said, who went through the war as Jews in France, there could not help but be a questioning of all accepted attitudes. That is why the longer I have lived in this country the more alien it has seemed to me, he said, because nowadays no-one seems to be aware any more of the real meaning of the events of the thirties and forties. Opportunistic uses of the Holocaust abound, he said, but real thinking on the subject is not only non-existent in this country, it is clearly never likely to take place, for the British, in the end, lived through a different war, the last heroic war, a war which only helped to reinforce the old myths of island solidarity and to encourage them later to turn upon those myths and imagine that they had got rid of them forever by showing them up for what they were. Hence, he said, the silly and superficial attacks on European Modernism by the old and the new puritans who cannot bear to experience contradiction and want only to feel that they are in the right. But what we have to do, he said as we fled from the Park and the cries of the caged animals and birds, is to live out the contradictions and to see what can be done with them. What I am after, he said as we waited at the bus-stop, is a work which tries to be generous to all contradictions, to place them against each other and let the reader decide. Even that, he said, is the wrong way of putting it. The reader too can only live out those contradictions, cannot adjudicate between them. And how many readers are prepared to do that? How many are willing to forgo the comfort of clear views, the balm of a narrative voice which tells them exactly where they stand? But what can I do? he said, that is just what I cannot provide, that is just what does not interest me. Each time, he said, it gets a little more difficult, each time I want to push out a little further, take the thing a little closer to the point of disintegration. Of course, if I take it too far I have lost, but if I hold back too much I have lost as well. The next time I saw him, exactly a week later, when we went for a walk in Epping Forest, he returned to his project. Swift, he said, like so many of the men of his time, was fascinated by the idea of a universal language. The reason in his case was his very modern feeling that he could not, in the language at his disposal, talk about what really mattered, what he really felt. But a universal language, in his mind, would be a language of the spirit, a language of the body, a language of birds and beasts, in which pain and desire could be uttered and so finally laid to rest. At the same time, he said, Swift was deeply sceptical of the notion and too much in love with the vagaries and varieties of English idiom and the registers of the English language. A part of him sensed that the language he had was the only language he would ever have and that he should make do with that. Not for him the romantic notion that there lay feelings in his breast buried too deep for words.

Gabriel Josipovici   121

Not for him Pope's 'Adieu, I can say no more, I feel so much.' So long as he could speak, so long as he could align words on a page, he saw no reason why he should not say what he wanted. And when he could no longer do so it was not the fault of language or of the depths of his feelings, but the result of his giddy fits and his loss of memory brought on by time. In 1736, when he is almost seventy, he writes to Pope 'I can as easily write a poem in the Chinese language as my own. I am as fit for Matrimony as Invention.' He has plenty of ideas for essays still, he says, but cannot write more than half a dozen lines. And then, six years later, total silence descends: I am what I am. Not because words cannot convey what he feels but because he cannot find the words. And yet, he said, his love of masks, his extraordinary way of piling irony on irony, testify to his feeling that beyond the language men ordinarily use there is another, lying in the interstices of that language so to speak, and which cannot be brought fully out into the open, only made manifest by indirection. His anger and despair, he said, lay in this contradiction, that he could only speak with ease when he donned a mask and yet he hated the thought of hypocrisy and cowardice and wanted to tear the mask off as soon as it was on. Why I thought of Moor Park as a title, he said, is that, like Animal Languages, it is a contradiction in terms, and I like titles like that. A park is precisely what is not moor, he said, what has ceased to be moor, nature, and has become park, civilisation. A moor, he said that day in Epping Forest, is nature without boundaries. A park, on the other hand, is precisely the imposition of boundaries, it makes human what was once natural. All books, he said, are moor parks, whether they realise it or not. Most, of course, do not. They think of themselves or their authors think of them as *either* moors *or* parks, either raw or cooked. What I have been trying to do in my book, he said, what my book, which is now at last, after all these years, nearing completion, twenty years or more of thought, ten years of writing, what my book is trying to be is a moor park or a park moor. Gardens are like books, he said, but they are in many ways more complex than books. For a garden is artificial but it is also natural. I cannot make a plant grow by an effort of will, even though I can ensure that conditions will be favourable for its growth. On the other hand I can order my garden in such a way as to express whatever I want. In my book, he said as we emerged from the wood in which we had been walking and found ourselves on the edge of a small lake, in my book Moor Park is, at different times, as I have explained to you, the home of Sir William Temple and his widowed sister, Swift's inveterate enemy, Lady Giffard, a school, a lunatic asylum, a college of theology, a centre for the decipherment of codes during the Second World War, a centre for the study of primates and again a school. The problem has been to hold all this together, he said, not through plot, for I have always been suspicious of plot, but through form. I have used a variant of the Fibonacci series to control the number of parts in the book, he said, and the number of sections in each part, and I have used palindromes, broken here and there according to further rules, to determine the relative length of each section. The themes, of which there are six – Swift, ciphers, monkeys, gardens, madness and language – make their appearance in accordance with the principles of the sestina, upon which I have superimposed another sestina, made up of the six subsidiary themes of love, masks, folly, age, boundaries and food. We took a path that seemed to lead round the lake. Epping Forest in the spring is full of the sound of birds and he kept on stopping and putting a hand to his lips to enjoin silence, then striding on, throwing the words over his shoulder. The idea of the park goes back to the Roman villa, he said. The big house is the focus and surrounding it are formal gardens, kitchen gardens, orchards and forest. The traditional park, he said, includes both wild and cultivated land, the whole enclosed within high walls, an image of the cosmos as the lord to whom it belonged conceived of it. I have also tried to use, as a sort of refrain, the image of a white figure thrashing about in a white room, a trussed up madman in an underground cell who is the spirit of all that is not and cannot be said in the book and perhaps even the source of the whole monstrous edifice, my alter ego, so to speak. This figure is silent throughout, but he hurls his trussed up body against the walls, the door, the window of his cell, and his movements, though to him they are merely the product of a violent and desperate urge to get free, form a sort of choreography which enacts the themes of the book, for the reader who is prepared to work a little. From time to time the figure will utter, from deep down in his throat, a series of cries or groans. As I said, he said, the whole of what is happening in the book may perhaps be happening in the mind of this figure, who has interiorised the history of the house, the life of Swift, the training of the apes. Perhaps he thinks of himself as Swift, darting in his imagination through Swift's life from the time at Moor Park when he taught the young Stella to read and write to the time when, as an old man living alone in his large rectory with a handful of servants he kept falling down the stairs, picking himself up and falling again, until he had to be confined to his bed and even tied down there. Moor Park, he said, or Animal Languages. I do not like the sound of the latter title, he said that day in Epping Forest, although I like its semantic content. On the other hand I do not care for the meaning conveyed in the first instance by Moor Park, it sounds too much like a work of history or perhaps a Regency romance, but I like what happens when you start to think about the two words separately and together. Every morning he said, sitting down under a tree, I am filled with despair. I am at my desk, eager to advance, and yet feel I cannot go forward. On the other hand, he said, the growing pile of pages under my hand is proof that I have tapped a vein and a rich one at that. My greatest fear, he said, is that it will give way under me. That the underpinning is not solid enough. That I have been on the wrong track from the start. Yet it is still growing, he said, and it has not yet collapsed, after all these years. It is very difficult to write when you are alone, he said. You ask yourself all the time why you are doing it and if, like me, you are deeply suspicious of the notion of inspiration and of the notion that there is something you have to say to the world, then the temptation to turn to something more obviously worth doing is very great. On the other hand, he said, it is quite impossible to write when you are not alone. It is impossible to write when there are other people around you all the time who feel they can make demands on you whenever they feel like it, at whatever time of the day or night. The trouble with me, he said, is that I have classical aspirations but a romantic temperament. I not only like but believe in the notion of regular daily work, of there being no question without an answer, no problem without a solution. But when it comes to it I cannot work unless I am fired by a belief in what I am doing, and there are many questions to which I have not been able to find the answer, many works I have started with high hopes and then been forced to abandon because I was unable to find the right solutions or even to decide what such solutions might be like if I should find them. But that is what we have to live with, he said, and got up abruptly and we left the lake and plunged once more into the birchwoods. Swift would have known what I am talking about, he said. He called for the formation of an academy to monitor English usage and outlaw unacceptable forms of speech but what he loved above all was the quirky, the phoney and the outrageous. He kept his fiercest satire for those Puritans who tried to speak in the language of the angels and succeeded only in uttering platitudes, yet *A Tale of a Tub* could be said to consist entirely of silences followed by grotesqueries. But at least he had political tracts to write when he had nothing better to do, he said. Not that he would have seen it like that, he was too much a man of his time not to feel that the political tract was of vital importance. As in his hands of course it was. How he saved Ireland again and again from the hasty, greedy and ill-thought-out schemes the English government kept trying to impose on it against its will is now a part of history. And of course he had thought at first that it was political tracts which would establish his reputation and allow him to live in the way he felt he was entitled to in the country of his choice – England. But it was not to be. Chance and the death of the Queen ruined his hopes. One could almost say that works like *A Tale of a Tub* and *Gulliver's Travels* were the ones which were written when there was nothing better to do. Nothing better to do, he said. Think of that. Think about it. But the individual works do not matter much, he said, the important thing, from my point of view at least, is that Swift wrote constantly, felt miserable when he was kept from doing so by illness or church business, and in the end all his works are one, the joke poems exchanged with Delaney, the histories, the satires, the tracts, the odes, the *Directions to Servants* and the *Polite Conversations*. Perhaps, he said, he imagined at times that Stella or perhaps Vanessa would make life bearable for him, but even as he thought this he must have known that if he chose to live with one or other of them just the opposite would happen and life would be even more unbearable than it already was. Monkeys are spared these choices, he said, but can we talk about an animal being *happy* as opposed to its being *contented*? He had talked about this before, notably on a walk we took along the Embankment from the Festival Hall to Tower Bridge. I have no experience of monkeys, he said, but I have had a great deal of experience of dogs and cats, and I am still not sure if the distinction can be made between happiness and contentment where animals are concerned. There is no doubt that they are miserable in captivity, no matter how well they are treated. And what about the chimps and gorillas? What about Lucy and Nim and Koko and the rest? Why should they have to learn to speak our language when they get along perfectly well without? Language arises out of need, he said, it is not an adjunct to gracious living. Why should not their so-called teachers learn from them rather than the other way around? In fact, he said, in my book one of the research projects under way at the Moor Park Primate Research Centre is precisely this, a scientist examining what it would take to turn a human into a chimp. The trouble is, he said, as when you go down on all fours and bark at your dog, the chimps only regard her with disdain and a faint amusement. Only an American, he said, would think of such a thing, and, having thought of it, try to carry it out. An American or a behavioural scientist, he said. The head of the Institute, he said, an English scientist of the old school, does not approve, but she has raised funding from a number of American agencies, and he is in effect powerless to stop her. She becomes so obsessed with her project, he said, that her marriage breaks down, not surprisingly, since her husband is finding it difficult enough to live with one chimp and naturally feels aggrieved to find that he has in effect now to live with two. When he suggests to his wife that she is becoming obsessive she accuses him of treating her like an animal and when, a week later, he returns to the subject, she responds to him only with grunts and groans, a bit of chest-beating and some remarkably accurate spitting. The real error these people make, he said, is to confuse speech and communication. Even human beings do not really communicate much through speech, groups, and couples in particular, develop a whole array of non-verbal signals and signs which are meaningless to outsiders but perfectly intelligible to them. In 1973, he said, two chimps, Ludwig and Bertrand, who had been used by the Moor Park Primate Centre to study the problem of language acquisition in children but who had proved recalcitrant and even, occasionally, violent, were transferred to Bristol. The Moor Park Institute was being severely reduced anyway because funding had dried up as a result of the lack of success of too many of the projects, and the much larger Institute of Behavioural Sciences in Bristol offered to give them a home. Unfortunately they seem to have torn off their name tags in transit and when they arrived in Bristol no-one could tell who was who. The Bristol people tried the direct approach, signing to one: Are you Ludwig? to which he replied with a prompt Yes. But when they asked the other if *he* was Ludwig he also said yes. The scientist who had been in charge of them at Moor Park had returned to America when the project was wound up, and the two assistants, on being summoned to Bristol to identify the chimps, disagreed as to who was who.

In a sense it no longer mattered, as the two chimps were now introduced into a colony established on a small artificial island at the Bristol Institute, where what was being studied was the social interaction of the monkeys, not their individual skills. So Bertrand and Ludwig lost their names and their identities and no-one has ever been able to re-establish them. Are they happier that way? Or less happy? And do such questions have any meaning? The book, he said, consists of 123 sections, and it will be divided into seven parts, forming a palindrome, a form I have used before in smaller works. The engineering problems, so to speak, he said, are not ones I have ever had to cope with before. But it is coming along, I learn as I go, and I do not think that I have more than a year's work ahead of me. What I will do when it is finished I simply do not know, he said. I have never had to face that question before, but in the last few months it has began to loom over me as I see the end ahead. This book has been my lifeline, he said, without it I could not have kept going all these years. I suppose I will have to face the situation when I come to it, he said, but I find it ironic that for eight or nine years, perhaps longer, I have dreamed only of making this thing, and dreamed too of having it off my back at last, and now that the end is in sight I am seized with a kind of blind panic. How do you explain it? he said. What is it that drives us like this and then leaves us in the lurch? I may be being optimistic though when I say I can see it being done in a year. I may be being pessimistic when I say the thought of the end drives me to distraction. On the other hand, he said, it may be done much sooner, I am rushing so fast towards the end that at times I am afraid I may overshoot it. As an old man, he said, Swift used to exercise by running up and down the stairs when the weather was too bad to go out. He would run up the front stairs of the rectory and then run down the back stairs, then up the back stairs again and down the front stairs. sometimes as many as seventy climbs and descents. His housekeeper and cousin in those last years, Mrs Whiteway, tried to restrain him but the old man was used to having his own way. Up and down he went, up and down, up and down, he said, and suggested we give South-wark Cathedral a miss. When he was younger of course, he said, Swift was one of the great walkers of English literature. We tend to think of Wordsworth and Coleridge and even Keats as the great walkers, he said, but Swift would have been a match for them, perhaps not for Coleridge but certainly for Keats. When he was writing his letters home to Stella every week, he said, he made a point of telling her that he walked home whenever he could from the City to his lodgings in Chelsea, a walk of at least an hour, 'for my health', he said. The cellars at Moor Park, he said, all give on to the back and have iron bars fixed to the windows. That is where the mad were kept. That is where the man in the white straitjacket was kept in his white room. For how long? And why? Who knows. He has no watch, and even had he had one it would have been of no use to him, time as we know it no longer means anything to him. Or to the chimps of course. But to the cipher-breakers of World War II, the old men suddenly finding themselves useful again, the young women linguists, the crossword geniuses and the mathematicians seconded from Cambridge, time was of the essence. A delay of a few hours and a whole fleet could be sunk out in the Atlantic. As Britain battened down the hatches and waited for America to make up her mind, in Moor Park the cipher wizards shut out the daily horrors and got on with their work. There were periods of rest of course, for no-one can work flat-out all the time, the basements with their barred windows which had once housed the mad were turned into billiard rooms and ping-pong rooms, the billiard room proper where once perhaps Sir William Temple had relaxed with his friends was taken over by the colonel in charge of the entire operation. Down there the young ladies played ping-pong with the mathematicians and half a dozen of them even inter-married after the war, one pair is still together. These cellars and base-ments, he said, when the house had become a primate research institute in the sixties and seventies, housed some of the complicated monitoring equipment and the mountain of files. But the English public, more sceptical than the American, never liked the idea of chimps being taught to use language. It was fine for Gavin Maxwell to keep an otter in his bath or for a retired bank manager to keep an eighteen foot boa-constrictor in a hothouse in Littlehampton, but the public objected to good research money being spent trying to teach chimps to talk when everyone knew perfectly well that what they would say if they ever did learn to sign was 'Koko want out' and 'Please Mick Lucy free'. If the higher apes have got by for a few million years without language why should we try and press it upon them? It's not as if they are going to be given the vote tomorrow. When we stop treating them as second-class citizens, when we extend the same legal rights to them as to human beings, then it'll be time to teach them to speak, or rather time for them to think about learning to speak. For the man in the white straitjacket in the small white barred room, he said, Swift and Stella are just beginning their lesson in the gazebo, Major Stanley is just rushing through the door into the billiard room waving a piece of paper in his hand, the pasty-faced youths in their drab suits are just opening Marshall's *Manual of the Aramaic Language*, edited by J. Barton Turner and with an introduction by Dr A. Mingana, Rabbi Abba bar Zabina, in the name of Rabbi Zera, said: 'If our ancestors were the sons of angels, then we are the sons of men. If they were the sons of men, then we are he-asses.' Rabbi Mani said in that hour: 'They say: Even to the she-ass of Rabbi Phinehas be Jair we will not liken ourselves.' Ab, father, abar, to be lost, abdalah, the benediction at the close of the Sabbath, abtiuna, a commissary, a Roman quartermaster, a lictor, abtikha, a melon, abel, to mourn. In the same billiard room, he says, rows of children, many of them Asian, are sucking their pens while one of them, brighter than the rest, begins to write: 'This is the istry of Moo Pak. This is the istry of Moo Pak owse and of Moo Pak gans. Bilt in the midle of the seveteeth sentry bai Sur Wim Temle –' He stops and sucks his pen, leaving a purplish mark on his lips to match those already covering his right thumb and index finger and the palm of his left hand. This is the istry. This is the istry. Can we guess at all what Stella thought of the whole thing? he said as we went into the Continental Buffet at London Bridge Station. Was she so submissive that she simply did what Swift told her? Was he so attractive that she was willing to do anything at all to keep him? If only she had left a diary like Alice James, he said, but in a way what is wonderful is that she didn't. There is a curious absence of sexual passion in both her and Swift, but that is more probably the result of what was considered fit to be written down in the eighteenth century as compared to the nineteenth. Of course if they were really half brother and sister the whole relationship needs reassessing. But are we really in the world of Byron here? However much one wants to criticise the Thatcher years, however ridiculous one may find the new British Rail policy of calling passengers customers, one has to admit that the opening of these Continental Buffets in most London main line stations is a plus, he said, and asked me if I wanted a croissant. Not quite what you get on the real continent, he said, but better than doughnuts. On the other hand, he said, there is no limit to what human beings will take to so long as it is new. Look at the popularity of hamburger joints in Paris, he said. And when my aunt was in London a few years ago, before these new continental buffets came in, she would walk all the way to Victoria Station to buy their disgusting cardboard sandwiches because she found that she had never tasted anything so delicious. When I first came to England, he said, nothing seemed tastier than Heinz baked beans followed by a cup of Horlicks. One of the reasons I gave up teaching, he said as we left the station, is that I feared we would soon have to start addressing our students as customers. That is what happens when the liberal consensus breaks down, he said. Into its place rushes first ideology and then, when that is bankrupt, money. The fear of authority and authoritarianism which has swept through America and then Britain is quite frightening, he said as we carried on along the embankment in the direction of Tower Bridge. It is no longer a question of teacher and pupil, he said but of seller and buyer. But when you are teaching literature what does a customer mean? I never thought I would give up on the world, he said, I always imagined my innate optimism would see me through. But everywhere I turn I find it more loathsome than before, everywhere I turn the values I believed in without even being aware of it are being quietly jettisoned and in their place there is only naked aggression and money. How long can a society exist when it is driven by such an engine? he said. How long can it survive when the only values it recognises are power and money? We have to turn our eyes away from these things, he said, and go on doing the things we believe in. But it grows harder and harder when what we believe in seems to be so much at odds with the way the world is going. And yet, he said, when I sit down at my desk and enter the world of Moor Park, the world of Animal Languages, all these doubts and despondencies drop away. In the end, he said, one writes for the people one loves and for oneself. Very often, he said, I have begun work on something with great excitement and great confidence only to find it collapsing under me because when the crunch came I did not really need it as much as I thought I did. Until you find out exactly where the real need is, he said, and just what will satisfy it, you cannot write anything worth while and, in my case, you cannot in fact write anything at all. We had reached Tower Bridge and begun to walk across it. In the old days, he said, I would take a boat down to Greenwich and walk in the park there. Now the sight of what they have done to the docklands depresses me so much I cannot bear to take the boat even though I still love Greenwich Park. Everywhere you go, he said, you see these new buildings made out to look like old buildings by the addition of little circumflex accents over the windows on the top floor. To call such architecture undistinguished, he said, is to betray the English language. It shames me, he said, to belong to a society which can perpetrate this kind of thing. When I am at the cinema, he said, and I find the film I am watching contemptible, which is most of the time, I get up and walk out because I feel that by staying

I would be conferring my own small sanction upon it. And it is the same with plays and operas. To sit through a play which offends your ethical and aesthetic sense is to deny that ethical and aesthetic sense, to get up and leave is not merely a gesture, it is a liberation. But you cannot walk out of a whole society, he said, especially as there is no other society to go to which is not bound to be as bad if not worse. The answer is perhaps to stay in your own room and let the world go to hell, but that is no answer either, for then you might as well be dead. I have been walking much at night recently, he said. I have been walking through the streets of London, letting my feet take me where they will. And it has to be said that at night things look much better, at night you can get the feel of a city and forget the hideous architecture and the hideous so-called improvements which have sprung up all over the place. But even at night, he said, you are either walking in suburbs which seem quite dead or in centres which seem to be thronged by frenzied revellers in search of enjoyment. Never by revellers enjoying themselves, such as you see in Rome and Paris and Prague and Munich, but only by those in search of enjoyment, by those with money in their pockets and no idea what to do with it, or else by those with nothing in their pockets and despair on their faces. Nobody seems to know how to live in cities any more, he said, they only seem to descend on cities in order to 'have fun' or to 'have a night out', as they would go to Whipsnade Zoo or Brighton pier in order to 'have fun' or 'have a day out' with the children. We cannot seem to live naturally in cities any more, he said, and we cannot live naturally in the country any more. The worst-off live on estates, so-called, made up of soulless disintegrating high-rise blocks, and the better-off live on estates, so-called, made up of tasteful semi-detached and detached villas, all with the same circumflex accent on the top-floor windows. Only the parks have not changed, he said, and only in the parks of the big cities, especially London, is it possible to feel alive. Last month we took a bus to Richmond and walked through the Park to the ponds. We watched the dogs running into the water to retrieve the sticks their owners had thrown for them. His mood was sombre, reflecting the August skies. I never felt like this before, he said. I might feel gloomy for a while but then I always blamed myself. Now, he said, I tend to blame the world. Is it that the world has changed or that I have? Or is it that I fear what will happen to me once the book is done? That is the trouble, he said, with living on your own. You cast aside everything that could be an impediment in your search and then of course you have nothing to fall back on when the search is over or lets you down. For ten years, he said, I have lived only for this book and for the completion of this book. If I thought about it at all I thought I suppose that I would die like Proust and Kafka, correcting proofs. Now I have to face the fact, he said, that I may live on with nothing new to make and no more proofs to correct. I can see myself already, he said, walking the streets and parks of London, talking to myself or inventing interlocutors to talk to, charming deferential people who listen and ask and show an interest, or sitting at my desk and writing about our walks and talks because I can no longer make anything that will stand up. What has happened to those two poor chimps, Ludwig and Bertrand? Do they search their memories for the names that once conferred selfhood upon them? Or are they happier for having forgotten them? Can we talk about happiness in connection with them? I had dreamed, he said, of writing a novel that would be as beautiful as Giusto Utens' lovely pale paintings of the Villa Medici and the Villa Lante at Bagnaia and the Villa Petraia at Florence, with those wonderful soft pinks and greens and the charming way house, formal gardens and wild park relate to each other and interact. Those paintings of Utens, he said, also remind me of the illustrations of books I read as a child and the happy days I spent immersed in them. Every detail clear, he said, and yet the whole impossible for the mind to take in. It would be a garden and a park, he said, and it would also be an *aide-mémoire* of the kind discussed by Frances Yates, a guide to the past that never existed or existed perhaps only in this book. A man cycled up on an old bicycle with a wooden box tied to the carrier. He got off, opened the box and let out a little dog, who immediately began to run round in circles. When you have been working on something for almost ten years, he said, it becomes a part of your life, you cannot separate it from what you have been through and experienced in that time, its pages inevitably evoke the days and weeks in which they were written, cold days and hot days, rainy days and sunny days, days when your head was clear and days when it was dull and empty. The man laid the bicycle down on the grass, looked round for a stick, found one and threw it into the pond. The dog ran in after it and soon only the top of his head and his nose were visible as he paddled furiously after the stick. The ducks dispersed, squawking. There are times, Jack said, when you forget what it's all for, why you started in the first place and where it is you are going. Then he stopped and we watched the dog, who had caught the stick in his mouth and was paddling back to the bank with it. Throughout our lives, he said, we are haunted by languages we can't quite decipher, can't quite hear. Hence the fairy-tales about magic rings which give you access to the language of birds and beasts. But even those closest to us, he said, speak a language we can never quite understand. Always, he said as the man picked up the stick the dog had laid at his feet and threw it into the pond again, much further than before, the most important things do not get said or get said in the wrong way. Always, he said. I have written in order to squeeze out the confusions, the evasions, as one squeezes water out of a towel. Not to say something but to clear the air so that something might be said. I have never succeeded, he said as we turned away and began to walk round the ponds. My words have been clumsy and every sentence I wrote, instead of standing there like a stone, has only carried the echoes of my own querulous and sometimes petulant voice. That is I suppose why one keeps trying again and again, he said. One always hopes to arrive at a voice which has nothing to do with oneself, which is, somehow, radically other than the one which one uses every day for the simple transactions of that day. But of course one never does, he said. We walked away from the ponds through the fern and the heather. The deer were nowhere in sight. I have dreamed sometimes, he said, of writing a book that would have the immediate impact of the cool wet nose of a big dog. That would touch others as I have been touched by all the many dogs in my life. Perhaps I will dedicate my book to them, he said as we emerged from the ferns onto a new path. I have often thought of having another dog, he said, but a dog needs a family just as every family needs a dog. You cannot have a dog on your own, he said, it's not fair on the dog and it's not fair on you. But the funny thing is, he said, that when I wake up in the night nowadays what I miss is not the familiar weight of my wife lying next to me but the familiar weight of a dog at the foot of the bed. Perhaps, he said, it has to do with the degree of trust which a dog reposes in you. There are those, he said, who argue that the relationship between man and dog is unhealthy and sentimental, that it allows the human being to exert control over a creature who does not make emotional demands on him which he would be unable to meet. People who say this sort of thing, he said, are like the people who say they can see no point in twenty grown men kicking a ball about for ninety minutes. Everybody these days knows how to detect inadequacy and failure in the emotional lives of others, he said. Unfortunately this does not make them any more human themselves or any more capable of bringing happiness to others. We reached Richmond Gate and walked down the road to the bus-stop. I am sometimes seized with wonder, he said, when I think of myself standing like this at bus-stops with you or with others or by myself in this or that part of London or its environs. Who would have imagined it? Why am I here? What am I doing? What steps have led a Sephardic Jew from Egypt to this spot and no other at this moment and no other? What I like about my machine, he said, my animal languages machine, my Moor Park machine, is that there is room in it for chaos and yet that it manages to function. Or rather, what I like about it is that at every moment it risks collapsing, bursting into a thousand pieces, but despite this it holds together. A work which holds together too easily is of no interest, he said. Ditto a work which falls apart at the slightest touch. The best works, or at least the works which please me best, are those which exist in such a state of tension that at every second we expect them to fly apart but at every second we are amazed because they do not fly apart. This is the istry of Moo Pak. I continue in an ugly state of health by the disorder in my head, which blister upon blister and pills upon pills will not remove, and this whole Kingdom will not afford me the medicine of an unfounded trotting horse. Swift to Pope, April 1732. Ludwig: Out out, come out me. Sidney Smith: I feel that the blue ape without a tail will never rival us in poetry painting and music. Eugene Rabinoff: Animal cries could never have evolved into intricate speech with its high information and low emotion content because they are controlled by different areas of the brain. Bertrand, looking at a photograph of a chimp resisting a bathtub scrub: Me cry there. In a few months it will be finished, he said as we stood by the round pond in Kensington Gardens. Then I will take a long holiday. The first I have indulged myself in for close on ten years. I will leave a copy with you, and another copy in the bank, and that will set my mind at rest. You may read it then if you wish to, but I know how busy you are just now and there will be time enough later. The worst way to read, he said, is with the thought that you do not have enough time. The only way to read is in the knowledge that there is an infinite amount of time stretching ahead, and that if one wishes to taste only a few sentences per day one is free to do so. Beckett used to come here, he said, when he was living in London in the thirties and going to the Tavistock for analysis and writing *Murphy*. This was the time when he almost went mad, he said, and the reason was that writing books like *Murphy* did not fully satisfy him and he did not know how to write any other kind. Perhaps, he said, it is when an artist is struggling most violently to find his voice that he produces his most interesting work. When Beckett let go the way of writing which had led to the production of 'Dante and the Lobster' and *Murphy* and *Watt*, when he let English go and began to write in a language that was not his own, let everything go and began to inch his way forward towards something completely new in the *Trilogy*, which of course was not a trilogy when he was writing it – only then did Beckett become Beckett. I sometimes think, he said, that Beckett's later work, like his early work, when he was secure in his style and method, is perhaps lacking in the tension necessary for true greatness. But only sometimes. At others I can only gasp in wonder at the quality of these late pieces. And it is the same with Nabokov. The novels he wrote when he first switched from Russian to English, *Sebastian Knight*, *Pnin*, *Lolita*, and before he had become a famous English writer and was no longer an interesting Russian writer, have got something that is missing in both the early and the late work. A quality of vulnerability, of wonder, which is as precious as it is rare. But that's how human beings are, he said, they will do everything to avoid pain, even the bravest of them. Yet we probably only find ourselves when we accept pain and doubt and uncertainty. The art of the past, he said, is only there to be used. If it is of no use to us then the best thing we can do is ignore it. That is the trouble with teaching literature, he said, it is based on the premise that literature is a valuable cultural commodity, whereas its only value is as a door leading each of us into the house he desires to inhabit. Bertrand, of course, did not *say*, Me cry there, he *signed* it. But that makes it even more heartrending. I am thinking, he said as we started to walk round the pond, of using it as an epigraph to the novel. For who is *me*? Bertrand when he signs? Swift? Stella? Ludwig robbed of his name and identity? The man in the white straitjacket hurling himself at the white padded walls of his cell? The person who has written it all? Or the person who reads it? Or the person who is at this moment talking to you? Bertrand looks at a photograph, he said as we approached the Albert memorial, and he signs in the language of the deaf. But what do we do when we write? Or paint? Or compose music? We look at the world and we listen to ourselves and we put down the signs we have learned. In fact, he said, I am just beginning to understand *me cry there* and see that it is in fact the central theme of the book, dispersed through its seven hundred pages, and my hope is that in reading it the reader will be able to take in the implications of the words, which are, after all, what the whole book is finally about. For the curious thing about feeling is that we do not feel *here*, we feel *there*, and even when we cry it is more perhaps at the sense of the dispersal of the self which is simply what life is, but which we usually keep from ourselves, than at any one thing, however painful, which has happened to us. As we cry, he said, we sense our dispersal and crying lets us accede to that dispersal and in crying we learn to accept it and live with it. Dispersal, he said, that is what I have always written about. But to write is to bring together, so that what we want to do and what we do never match up but come into inevitable conflict as soon as we start. Perhaps though, he said as we entered the Serpentine Gallery, this is something my machine has at last allowed me to say and enact. Crying and laughing, he said, that is what defines our humanity, and yet that is what art never quite seems able to express and enact. The gallery was between shows and the exhibition rooms were closed off. We went out again and sat down on a bench in the little garden that stands between the gallery and the road. It is easy enough to say it, he said, but to say it is to deny it, so you have to find a way of enacting it. I do not think I have succeeded in doing this till now, except perhaps in a few small pieces for the stage and radio and perhaps in the occasional short story. I had always suspected, he said, that the only way to do it was by writing something very big, but I had never seen how to do it. But pressure, he said, is the only spur to creativity. I wrote my first work under the pressure of fear, he said, the fear that I would never be able to write anything more than five pages long. And now the pressure of feeling that time is after all running out has led me through my doubts and

Gabriel Josipovici 139

inhibitions and out the other side. I wonder, he said, if it has always been like that, if the author of *Pearl* and Shakespeare himself, who seem so relaxed, so comfortably in control, only in fact produced good work when some unknown and forever unknowable pressure was upon them. At the same time, he said, we have to think of art as a natural activity and to engage with it in a spirit of freedom and disinterestedness. Yet only Shakespeare and Mozart have, he said, ever been able satisfactorily to combine the heart-rending and the lighthearted. All the rest, when you think about it, he said, is more bad than good, more a cause for despair than for celebration. Nothing makes one feel so ill, he said, as the sight of immense effort brought to bear on the wrong things and in the wrong spirit, and that, unfortunately, is what must be said of the bulk of human art. That is why I applaud Frank Auerbach's remark that Delacroix's *Turkish Bath* is good but a turkish bath is better. That is why I deplore our modern and romantic obsession with art and creativity and why I prefer the Serpentine Gallery as we have found it today to what it would have been like had an exhibition been on view. But the tactic of Duchamp and his followers is no sort of answer, he said, in typical modern and romantic vein it is based on a half-baked idea and a conceptual fallacy that a twelve-year-old would have no trouble seeing through if our society had not brow-beaten him into imaginative blindness. Only gardens, he said, escape such criticism, only gardens and perhaps poems such as those of Wallace Stevens which make art of precisely such a contradiction. No reputable linguist today, he said, would dream of developing a theory about the origins of language, just as no nineteenth-century linguist would have dreamed of tackling any other subject. The nineteenth century, he said in the little garden in front of the Serpentine Gallery, thought you could explain everything in terms of its origins. Naturally it developed theories about the origins of language along with theories about the origins of man, culture and the universe. Language, it was thought, grew out of the grunts of animals. It grew, another theory went, out of the need for men to plan ahead if they were to hunt successfully. And so on and so forth. Today, he said, a number of facts have been established which help to move the discussion forward. First of all there is the simple matter of the ape's vocal chords. Only a being which stands upright can keep its vocal chords free enough to utter the variety of sounds which make up human speech. That is why apes have been taught language in the form of the sign language of the deaf. The daughter of Thomas Mann, he said, once informed the world that her dogs wrote poetry. They would press the keys of a special typewriter she had invented for the purpose with their noses. Unfortunately the examples of their poetic skill which she reproduces in her book fail to convince. On the other hand the typewriter she invented has proved extremely useful to handicapped children. Thus does technology advance. But since the work of Chomsky has taken hold, he said, and his suggestion that we have, built into the human brain, a blueprint for language learning which other species do not have, the spirit has rather gone out of all these experiments to prove that animals can, given the right environment, be taught to speak. But as I have said to you before, he said, my own feeling is that animals have all they need for their not very elaborate social lives, and though they do not have the *Critique of Pure Reason* to their credit, they do not, I suspect, feel the lack. In the course of my book, he said, the characters of two of the primate research workers are developed and many of the others sketched in. It will come as no great surprise to you, he said, that none of them finds it easy to communicate to his or her fellow human beings and most of them have even more difficulty communicating with themselves. This too, he said, is part of the istry of Moo Pak. On the other hand, he said, have you ever come across an animal who does not know what he wants? You may say that that is because his wants are simpler but that is to beg the question. Why should we have developed into the animal which does not know what it wants? And is that development in some way bound up with the use of language? Is it not possible then to see the development of human language as a sickness rather than as a source of pride? And does the same not hold for art? He got up and asked me if I wanted to walk round the lake before we parted. We forget Nietzsche's insights at our peril, he said as we waited to cross the road. On the other hand prolonged meditation on Nietzsche's favourite themes seems to have the effect only of driving one mad, as it drove him mad. Are we then reduced to the Swiftian alternative of either burying our heads in the sand or succumbing to madness and despair? he asked as we negotiated the traffic and arrived safely on the other side of the road. I have never believed that, he said, or at least not since I reached the age of twenty. What both Swift and Nietzsche tend to overlook and what they of all people should not have overlooked, he said, is the pleasure that making things gives us, the pleasure of the daily routine, the pleasure in the object well made, and surely such pleasures are as much a fact of human life as the desire for truth and the awareness of death. Is it, he said, that we Jews are naturally melancholic and driven by a need for truth and by an ethic of hard work, so that we will always lack the spark of pure playfulness to be found in a Mozart, a Picasso, a Queneau? When I wake up in the mornings though, he said as we rounded the pond and began to walk back in the direction of the bridge, and see the pile of typewritten sheets neatly stacked on the desk, to the right of my typewriter, I have to admit that my heart leaps and I have to pinch myself to make sure I am not dreaming. When I think back to its hesitant beginnings all those years ago, he said, to all those false starts and those weeks and months and even years of despair, of knowing that all that would save me was to write something bigger and more complex than I had ever written before and yet being unable to find a way to do it, I can hardly believe that it has arrived at this. I do not say that I have brought it to this, he said, because it does not seem to be a single person who has done it. Rather, he said, it has simply grown, as I have used my two hands to pound the keyboard of my old typewriter, day after day. And it has been able to grow, he said, precisely because it has so little to do with me, with my feelings or my thoughts. Of course, he said, if it had not been for me, for the hours I put into it every day for all these years, there would have been no pile of sheets by now, but it has only grown because I found, at the start, a way to sever it from myself. All those false starts, he said, were nothing but the attempt to discover how such a severance should be made and they were false precisely because the severance was not radical enough. A piece of fiction which consists of reminiscence or preaching cannot stand up, he said. It is like a chair with only two legs. Those two may be very beautiful, they may have been lovingly made, they may embody the profoundest thoughts and feelings of the carpenter, but with only two legs no chair will stand up. The whole history of language and of human culture, he said, is to be found in the decision to renounce the immediate pleasure for the long-term benefit. Aaaaah to Ma-Ma, as Roman Jakobson has so well described it. The task of art, on the other hand, he said, is to find a way of returning to the Aaaah! but in such a way that it can be grasped by others, that it enters the sphere of the social. Is it a coincidence do you think, he asked, that both Jakobson and Chomsky are Jews? That Chomsky's first published work was on the Hebrew language? I am of course not suggesting that Hebrew was the original language or is closer to the origins of language than any other language, just as I am not suggesting that Jews were the first at anything whatsoever. I am only wondering out loud, as others must have wondered, though no-one has, to my knowledge, put such ideas into print, for obvious reasons. Nonetheless, he said, the power of Chomsky's work has perhaps retarded rather than advanced our understanding of the origins of human language. For, like so many other thinkers before him, but now in full awareness of what he is doing, Chomsky has found the means of cutting man off from his past and so from all other animals. There is a fierce rationality about Chomsky, he said, which more than one commentator, taking up hints in his own writing, has compared to that of Descartes. I myself, he said, prefer to see it as a Jewish trait, like the burning intellectual intensity of a Spinoza or a Wittgenstein. But if he is to be compared to Wittgenstein, he said, it has to be to the young Wittgenstein, for though Wittgenstein lost none of his intensity as he grew older he came to see that our confusions and failures are at least as important as our triumphs and successes and as much in need of explanation. Confusion for Descartes, on the other hand, he said, is something to be eliminated, much as Luther and Calvin wished to eliminate sin. But I am with the later Wittgenstein in this, Jack said, that I believe we eliminate sin and confusion at the cost of eliminating our humanity. On the other hand, he said, we should obviously not make a fetish of failure and confusion. What I have tried to do in all my work and above all in *Moo Pak*, he said, is to dramatise the interrelation of chaos and order, of confusion and clarity, of the desire to let go and the need to control. To give in to chaos, he said, is to give up the idea of art and knowledge altogether; to deny confusion and chaos is to produce something which bears no relation at all to what we are. That, he said, is the paradox and the challenge. The barking of dogs and the communal praise of God, the murder of millions and the individual's joy at the play of sunlight on leaves, the utter pointlessness of life and thanksgiving for being alive. Our art must reflect both or it is worthless and less than worthless, a hindrance to joy and understanding. He has become quieter in the past few months. When we walk he talks less about his book. He talks less altogether. He listens to what I say and seems happy to walk in silence. I know better than to ask him how the book is going, he has talked often enough about the difficulty of endings. When you start a book, he says, everything is open. You can take any path secure in the confidence that it will lead somewhere. The difficulty comes when you get to the middle, he says, and when you begin to lose faith in the project and in your ability to carry it through. You not only do not know if you can finish what you have begun but you cease to be sure that there is anything to finish. But if you can work your way through that, he says, then the long run home is the most enjoyable of all. You know that you will finish, even if you have had reluctantly to admit to yourself that what you will be finishing will be far from what you had envisaged when you started. But endings have their own particular problems, he says. For if there are a hundred ways to start there is only one way to end, and if you do not find that way then you put in jeopardy everything that has gone before. Often, he says, he has thought he has finished only to discover that he hasn't, or thought he has found the only right way only to discover that it wasn't. A book is like a life, he says. When we start becoming conscious of ourselves there are many directions in which most of us feel we can go and each of them seems equally valid. At the same time we are always confident that time is on our side and that if we find after a few years that we are on the wrong track we can always go back and start again. By the middle of our lives, he says, we are only too conscious of the fact that we have taken a false turning or any number of false turnings but we are too far forward to do anything but press on. But as we near the end of our lives, he says, and as we feel time growing short, we realise that every step must now be the right one because now there will certainly be no second chance. At the same time, he says, we must not panic, for panic can only paralyse us, we must keep doing well the things we know we can do and the things we know we have to do. It is the same with a novel, he says. And with this one in particular. I have been working at it too long to be able to start again and I have given up too much of my life to countenance the thought that it might be a failure. And yet, he says, if the ending is not right all that has gone before will fall back into the dust. Moor Park now exists for whoever reads the book, he says, with its fountains and hedges, its formal gardens and orchards, its lawns and stream and woods. Swift and Stella too, he says, and Sir William Temple and his sister Martha Gifford, the chimps Ludwig and Bertrand and the scientists at the Primate Research Centre, Helen and Peter and Mike and Abe. The schoolboy has rewritten his essay on the history of Moor Park half a dozen times and the German radio messages have been intercepted and decoded. In the white cell the white padded figure has hurled himself at the walls and door in vain and the history of the house in which he is in effect a prisoner has passed through his head and re-emerged in a thousand lurid variants. At his desk the author has watched his hand move over page after page, covering it in signs which he dreads to reread, and he has walked through the parks and heaths of London talking to himself as though to another until the last little section has fallen into place. This is the istry of Moo Pak. This is the istry a Sift an Sella. This is the istry a Ludy an Bertam. This is the istry a mad in cela an mad rite all pas in hed centries an centries an river an wood, pak an moo an shreek an smile al in on plaice an meny ears, wak in Lonen dak before an so dak after, all eye can do eye hev tride mai best. Now, he says only the few final pages are missing, pages which will write themselves if only one can hit on the correct angle. The time has long gone, he says, when one has to worry about the rightness of one's early decisions or even the reasons why one embarked on the project in the first place. The temptation, he says, is to believe that now one only needs to hang on and one will get to the end. But it is never a question of just hanging on, least of all at the end. There are always decisions to be taken, he says, everything can still be lost. When it is done, he says, then will be the time to worry about whether it should have been done at all. I have never seen him in quite this mood before. Even when he was working most intensely he would still only ask me to walk with him when he was in an expansive mood and even when nothing was going right with his work he would always have plenty to say about all sorts of other topics. When we look up from our desk, he says, we are done for. But if we never look up from our desk we are also done for. At the same time, he says, and despite all evidence to the contrary, I never really feel we are done for. That may be my Jewish optimism, he says, what distinguishes me from Beckett and Bernhard. That may be why I feel, however much I admire them, and I admire them greatly, that there is an element of play-acting about their work, which they would like to eliminate but can't, which they would like to eradicate but are secretly rather pleased with. I call that the Hamlet syndrome, he says, for just as Hamlet makes out that he is slightly madder than he is to try and convince himself that he is not mad at all, but succeeds in persuading neither himself nor us, so with Beckett and Bernhard. What I would like to do, he says, is to write and to live without play-acting but without undue solemnity either. The play-acting of Christians, of course, he says, is different from the play-acting of Jews. The play-acting of St Paul and Pascal and Kierkegaard, he says, is quite different from the play-acting of Jacob and of David and even of Jesus. The play-acting of Bergman is quite different from the play-acting of Woody Allen. The play-acting of Thomas Mann is quite different from the play-acting of Saul Bellow. There is a glint in the eye of Jacob, he says, even as he tears his clothes and laments the death of his beloved son Joseph. But Kierkegaard's eyes do not glint and neither do Mann's. Life is too grim for that and at the same time life is not grim enough. Let me go, they cry out, and that is the cry of Beckett and Bernhard as well, let me go and leave for ever this desert where I find myself. The Jew on the other hand, he says, knows that if he were to be lifted out of this desert by the hand of a God who had listened to his pleas he would only be set down in another desert, identical to the first. If that's the case, he says, then why not settle here and make the most of it? A little ingenuity and even the desert may be made to bloom. A little ingenuity, a little patience, a little trust, and even the desert may be made to bloom. Three weeks ago for the first time that I can remember he arrived late for our rendezvous. He had gone to sleep, he said, in the middle of the day and only just woken up in time to get to our place of meeting, the Legless Ladder in Battersea. I offered him a drink but he said he was impatient to be walking. When we got to the park he suddenly said his choice of venue had been a mistake and suggested we take a taxi to Hampstead Heath. In the taxi he told me there was no novel. I asked him what he meant and he said he had been talking and talking about it in the hope that it would materialise but that it hadn't and he had to face up to the fact that it never would. I was confused and asked him to explain. He said there were notes but no novel. He said that far from almost finishing it he had never really started it. Not that it matters, he said, it would not have worked even if I had written it. I asked him if he had been lying when he said he had written six or seven hundred pages. Yes, he said, he had written nothing at all. He repeated: a few notes and nothing else. In ten years? I asked. In ten years, he said. But why tell me now? I asked him. The taxi had got us to the pond at the top of Heath Street and we paid and got out. He said he had been hoping every day to make the breakthrough. He said that for years he had felt that it just needed one flash of inspiration for everything to fall into place, one little bit of luck for him to find a way to get it going. Everything was there, he said, all the separate elements, it was only a question of how to relate them to each other. Often, he said, I thought I had found the way, but it always turned out to be a mirage. It was as if, he said, there was a gauze screen between me and it, and by focussing hard, by sharpening up my vision, I would be able to see through the blur to the clarity behind. But I never did. Of course, he said, solutions came to me, but almost as soon as I thought of them they revealed themselves as meretricious. For ten years, he said, I felt sure that there was a genuine solution to the problems, one natural and inevitable way of doing it. But now, he said, I have had to face the fact that there isn't. Or at least that even if there is I will never be able to find it. He had wanted to tell me as soon as he had come to that conclusion. Besides, he said, I had begun to realise that it made no difference whether I ever wrote the thing or not. It would have made a difference to me of course, he said, but essentially it would have made no difference. I said it would have made a difference to me and he laughed. We ran down a sandy hillside into the Heath. It might have made a difference to you if I had never talked about it, he said. But not now. Now, he said, you only have to go away and write it yourself. He laughed. I had never seen him in such a strange mood. Last night, he said, as I lay awake, I could see it in the form of a ship, sailing away from me into an endless sea, throwing up spray as it went. It felt, he said, as though it was carrying the essential part of me with it and leaving me alone and empty on the shore. Perhaps there was a moment when I might have written it, he said, but that moment passed a long time ago. Perhaps what I envisaged was in the end not worth doing. Perhaps that is what I have been trying to conceal from myself for all these years. When I saw that ship go, he said, I felt bereft, but I also felt as though a weight had been taken off my back forever. I asked him what he was going to do now and he said he would go on doing what he had always done, read and walk and talk to his friends and think. Nothing has changed, he said, and laughed again. Nothing has changed. I knew in my bones ten years ago, he said, that it was all over with my writing. I did not want to face up to that truth. I went on trying to persuade myself that it was the temptation of the devil. And could it not still be the temptation of the devil? I asked him. Yes, he said laughing of course. But what can I do? he said, and looked at me helplessly. I have done what I could, he said. I have done what I thought right. I have lived according to my precepts. Of course I have done many foolish and reprehensible things. But at least where my writing is concerned I have always tried to be true to myself. When you are young, he said, you do not ask yourself too many questions. After the age of fifty, he said, you have got to ask yourself what you are doing with your life. I have gone on trying, he said, because there did not seem to be any alternative, or rather, because all the alternatives seemed worse than what I was doing. Perhaps he said, I should have been a doctor like my grandfather or a lawyer like my great-grandfather. There comes a time in life, he said when you ask yourself what use you have been to anybody, and I have to say my record is not one I am particularly proud of. Perhaps, he said, I was a reasonably good teacher, and in a system in which I had had more confidence might have gone on a little longer. I did at least, he said, give a few kids the sense that books were worth reading and could even be a source of high excitement. Perhaps, he said, I helped a few to have trust in their own instincts and not to take anything for granted or pay too much attention to any of the so-called experts. But I did not behave well towards my wife or, I suppose, my children. And while my own writing has given me satisfaction as I worked on it I cannot say it has done much for anyone else. And yet, he said, despite everything, and despite even the disaster of *Moo Pak*, I cannot quite accept that I was wrong to spend so long trying vainly to write it, and I cannot quite accept that I will never write again. It is a bleak prospect though, he said, when something that has lived with you all your conscious life and to which you have given the best of yourself eventually lets you down. The trouble is, he said as we walked through the autumn landscape of Hampstead Heath, that when I felt I was writing well, whether in fact I was writing well or not, I also felt that life was worth living and that I had a contribution to make, however small. In the last few months, he said, I have felt my horizons narrowing and my enthusiasm waning, and now it seems I have come to the end of the road. Then he said he had nothing else to say to me that day and we parted. He walked off in the direction of the ponds and I turned back to the bus-stop. That was three weeks ago. On Tuesday I received a note from him asking me to meet him today at the Star and Garter in Putney. I waited for over an hour, wrote Damien Anderson, and then, when it was quite obvious he was not going to turn up, I went home. I do not think he will send me any more messages. Why did he send me this one? Did he imagine our relationship could continue unaltered after what had happened at our last meeting? And did he then, when the moment came, find that it could not? I had known, I think, he wrote, without quite admitting it to myself, ever since that taxi-ride across London from Battersea to

Hampstead Heath, that this would happen and that then I would have to write down, however inadequately, my memories of my meetings with him and of what he had said to me on our walks. I think I had even known for some time prior to that, he wrote, that he was not really writing his book and that it would be left to me to put down what little I could recall of all he had said about it. But it is not the book I have wanted to write about, he wrote, it is the man. We did not meet very often and yet my life would have been the poorer if I had never known him and if we had never walked together in the parks and heaths of London between the winter of 1977 and the autumn of 1990. What does it mean to say that my life would have been the poorer? wrote Damien Anderson. Poorer in what sense? What does richness mean exactly when it does not refer to money? I do not know, he wrote. I only know that I am prepared to stand by what I have written here: my life would have been the poorer had I never known him and had we never walked and talked together for over ten years in the parks and heaths and along the waterways of London. Let that suffice.